Also by the author:

Story Collections:
A History of Things Lost or Broken

Novels:
The Bronx Kill
Dark Road, Dead End
Jesusville
Catholic Boys
If Anyone Asks, Say I Died from the Heartbreaking Blues

Film:
Love in the Age of Dion

Plays:
Love in the Age of Dion
Closing Night at the Paradise
Small Sounds Vanishing in the Dark

NIGHT AND ITS LONGINGS

Philip Cioffari

Livingston Press
The University of West Alabama

ISBN 13: trade paper 978-1-60489-374-8
ISBN 13: hardcover 978-1-60489-373-1
ISBN 13: e-book 978-1-60489-376-2

Library of Congress Control Number: 2023949081
Printed on acid-free paper
Printed in the United States of America by
Publishers Graphics

Typesetting and page layout: Joe Taylor, Cassidy Pedram
Proofreading: Brooke Barger, Savannah Beams, Raina Voss
Cover art and layout: Asha Hossain
Author photo: Ken Haas

Livingston Press is part of The University of West Alabama,
and thereby has non-profit status.
Donations are tax-deductible.

6 5 4 3 2 1

NIGHT AND ITS LONGINGS

PROLOGUE

New York City, 3 a.m.
July, 1995

This is the Nite Hawk, coming to you from the far end of your radio dial, 1660 AM, asking you:

What do we do with the night?

We sleep.

We dream.

We fall, then fall deeper.

Sea journeys on oceans stretched thin beneath black skies. Watery graves where past, present and future are buried as one. Where time is measured in moments lost, and the mind's eternal precipice is what passes for solid ground.

Images appear and recede. Shadows collide. Light becomes darkness, and darkness light. Until there is no difference.

And those who cannot sleep? Those of us upon whom night, with its distinctive calling card, has bestowed its personalized desolation?

We wander, wonder. What is real, what is not. . .?

Tonight's story comes to us from Jake, right here in the heart of the city . . . .

PART ONE

New York City, June 1995

1

One chance, that's how I saw it.

For love, the true kind.

One chance.

Play hard, play to win. You blow it, well, you spend the rest of your life alone. Or you drift, ghost-haunted, woman to woman. Which pretty much summed up my life since Vera and I split. I thought love, the enduring sort, had kissed me goodbye.

Past midnight, that's the way you think. The way *I* think.

I was hunched over the typewriter, re-reading the last lines I'd written: another of my hardboiled detective stories with what I liked to think of as a metaphysical edge. *The street was dark and empty. Morrison moved to the head of the alley. He hesitated before its long tunnel of shadows. He'd always been wary of dark places. Too many childhood nightmares. Memories, too. But he pushed those aside. He knew he had to face what awaited him—the gunman or one of his victims. And now he moved into the alley itself, snub-nosed revolver in hand. . .*

Downstairs someone was knocking.

No one came at this hour. Not even Connie, the woman I was seeing at the time. Yet the knocking continued.

From my window the caller was hidden by the leaves of a beech tree. What I *could* see was the courtyard below and the narrow alley, dark with shadow, leading to the street.

My door opened directly into the courtyard. Outside, framed against the newly green fluorescence of the beech, stood a man of medium build with thinning, sand-colored hair, his face partially in leaf-shadow. Leaning toward me. Hands shoved deep in his pockets. Shoulders trembling though it was a mild night that smelled of flowers and courtyard grass.

"How are you, Jake?" he said. "I deeply apologize for the intrusion at this ungodly hour, but I saw your light was on and—" He stared at me like a man clinging to a lifeboat. "And so I knew you were still up, still writing. You see, I've been here before, the past few nights, watching from the alley."

He stopped himself and shrugged in apology. "That sounds awful, I know. I'm sorry. I'm no stalker. It's just that. . .I could see you in the window, typing, so I knew—"

He left the sentence hanging and thrust out his hand. "It's Norm Davison."

It took a moment to connect the face to the man I'd known.

"Vera's husband," he said. "I didn't know who else to turn to."

2

Stunned, I stood there holding the door, ignoring the outstretched hand.

Ten years had taken off some weight, thinned his hair, narrowed the contours of his face. He wore glasses now. He seemed tentative, the way he held himself. Last time I saw him he wore the same disconcerted, helpless look. A man enduring the force of an avalanche.

"There's an all night café up the street," I said. "We can talk there." Given our history, no way did I want the man in my house.

The street was empty. The café, too. Dark as usual with its ebony woodwork and heavy wooden tables. Shadows that fell like mist. A place the remaining artist-types left in the West Village, and misfits of one sort or another, came to drift deeper into themselves.

A beer for Davison, double espresso for me.

The man took a long pull, tilting his head back and sucking greedily from the bottle. Setting it down squarely on the table, he said: "My nerves are shot to hell."

I knew him—the few times I'd been in his presence—as even-keeled, unflappable, abnormally so. Early fifties by now, older than Vera or me by more than a decade. A college prof—zoology—at NYU.

"I know it's strange," he was saying, "coming to you like this. You probably think I'm crazy. I wouldn't have done it if—" It appeared as if his doubts would prevent him from continuing. "If I didn't think—"

The clock above the counter hummed into the stillness. "It's Vera," he said. She's disappeared."

"What do you mean she's disappeared?"

"She said she was going to the park, never came back."

"When? How long ago?"

"Eleven days, to be exact. I've been out of my mind with worry. Pacing the floor, waiting for her to show up, waiting for the phone to ring, waiting for—*any*thing." He raised the bottle again, gulped hard. His face a roadmap of grief and worry; a barely concealed look of shame there as well, as sudden and abrupt as a detour. "The past few nights, as I've said, I've been outside your apartment, working up the courage to knock on your door."

"You thought she was with *me*?"

His face flushed. "I—I didn't know what to think—"

"Did you two have a fight?"

"No."

"Did she say anything about me?"

"Not recently, no."

"I haven't seen or spoken to Vera in ten years, if that puts your fears to rest." Though, given our history, the last thing on my mind was the need to offer the man any sort of consolation. I couldn't keep the resentment out of my voice. "She could have left you for me anytime since then, and she didn't. Why would she do it now?"

He shook his head in apology or maybe exasperation. "I've had too much time to think." He raised the bottle to drink again but held it in the air as if he'd forgotten what purpose it served, before setting it back down on the table. "I'm looking at every conceivable—"

"Forget it. Cross me off your list."

What he said next, even more than the fact of her disappearance, came at me like a closed fist.

"She never stopped loving you."

Silence, the past, hung like a wall between us.

"How do you know that?" was all I could stammer out in response.

"A husband knows. There doesn't have to be anything in particular he can point to. He just knows. He can feel it."

He fingered the beer bottle, turning it in slow circles on the table. "But there are things I *can* point to. The times she'd say your name in her sleep. When I'd ask if she'd been dreaming about you she'd say yes but she couldn't recall any of the details. Or there'd be times in bed when she'd get quiet and I'd ask her what she was thinking and she'd say, 'Nothing.' It didn't take me long to realize 'nothing' was a euphemism for *you*."

He stared at me, expecting something. But there were things for which one's life offered no preparation and this was one of them.

I'd always talked myself into believing Vera had moved on with her life, that—for her—our year together had fallen into the category of youthful passion, heart-strong and heedless. I told myself I should be pleased that she hadn't forgotten me—if it was true, if it wasn't some ploy he was using to manipulate me—but what I felt was something more like remorse and something even more difficult to define: a dark hope, a hurting more than an inspiration.

"I thought when she got pregnant, when she had the baby," Davison was saying, "things would be better, that she'd forget about you and focus on *us,* the family we were becoming." He stopped himself then, embarrassment or shame again coloring his face. "I'm sorry. Burdening you with my problems, *our* problems."

I winced at the word *our*.

"And for a while, things *were* better. Until last year when our child died."

Another gut-punch. I knew she was going to have a child but not that she'd lost one.

Davison leaned against the table, hands gripped tight to the bottle planted like an anchor on the scarred wood surface. "Then, as I've said, eleven days ago she didn't come home. I'm hoping you'll help me find her."

It seemed, in my unsettled state at the moment, like a plot I might have conjured up for one of my novels: cuckolded husband seeks wife's lover's help finding her when she mysteriously vanishes.

He waited before saying, "I think you're the key to her disappearance."

3

The silence felt like an assault.

I stared at him in disbelief. "How? How am I the key?"

He bowed his head in some form of resignation. "You just are. I know it."

"That's insane. I already told you I've had no contact with her all these years."

"Even so—"

This was absurd. Him coming to me like this. What degree of desperation, what extreme of panic would it take for a man to humiliate himself like this, asking for my help? After all that had happened. After the way things had ended between us. Or was he being manipulative again rather than desperate? Setting me up for something. Feeding me another lie, like the one before it: *I didn't know who else to turn to.*

"I don't want to get involved," I said. "My connection to Vera's a thing of the past." I gave him a pointed look. "No use raking through the ashes." But even as I said that in the dim stillness of the café it was obvious, to me at least, how transparent was the lie. "Your best bet's going to the police."

"I've been to the police."

"And—?"

It was his turn to give *me* a look, as if I should know better. "You're a crime writer, you—my point is you have some understanding of the criminal justice system. You know how many missing persons cases the NYPD gets each week?"

"A lot."

"Unless I can prove it was an involuntary disappearance—"

I knew the drill. The local precinct would investigate only what they considered "special categories" of the missing: the elderly, children under thirteen, the mentally ill, or victims of a crime. Otherwise they simply filed paperwork and passed it on to the Missing Persons Squad where it would receive even less attention. The MP Squad eventually turned it over to a state Clearinghouse. Where it would become one more statistic in their data base.

"They as much as told me it was a needle-in-the-haystack kind of thing," Davison said.

"A private investigator, then."

"That's an impersonal thing, a job. It's not the same as someone who cared about her." He downed more of his beer and glared at me.

"She's nothing to me now," I said. "She's—a distant memory. A stranger."

He called for another beer and leaned closer. "What if someone's trying to hurt her right now?" He pressed even closer to me. "She'd been on edge for days. These phone calls—they'd come at all hours. She'd be visibly upset. When I asked her about them, she never gave me a direct answer."

I've never responded well to someone laying a guilt trip on me, but this one set off reverberations in so many directions I couldn't sort them out. I couldn't think clearly. What I said, with an edge of bitterness, was: "She's taken care of herself without me all these years."

"This is different. Surely you can see that."

It wasn't quite hatred for the man, but an anger and resentment that came close, for his laying this at my feet. The truth of the matter, though, was something I couldn't admit. Fear of unearthing feelings long buried. Fear of opening old wounds.

"You've got the wrong person."

He looked at me with narrowed eyes. "Not the way I see it."

"That's no fault of mine."

He shook his head sadly. "I expected more of you."

What he meant, what his eyes gave away, was *You owe me. For what you did. You sure as hell owe me.*

I threw some bills on the table to cover our drinks and left him there.

4

Hudson Street, a late-night watering hole.

A double shot of Irish whiskey.

Davison's words turning over in my head: *I expected more of you.*

Yeah well, I thought, *I* expected more of myself too. I'd expected more of my *life.* More than ending up a less-than-famous writer. Short on money and friends. A blank page jammed into a typewriter for a future.

Expectations be damned.

Who doesn't expect more of himself? Expectations are one thing, real life is another.

The unavoidable truth was this: Vera had been thrust back into my life. The words I'd said to Davison came back to mock me. *She's a distant memory. A stranger.*

Who was I kidding?

She was the dead center of my sorrow.

Then the voices started up. The endless back and forth.

Your time's come and gone. You've lost the best thing you ever had.

There's always possibility. There's always hope.

For what?

Another beginning. A second chance.

The stuff of movies and books, romantic claptrap.

Things can change. A man's life can change.

In dreams, maybe.

As long as there's breath. As long as—

Another myth.

Myths are man-made. We can write new ones.

Can we? You've always been a loner. Of course you're short on friends. As for Vera, face it: you just weren't good enough.

I can be better. I can *learn* to be better.

Dream on.

I can.

Yeah, like your compatriots here. Look around you. What do you see? Any new myths here? Anybody getting better?

What I saw was a down-at-the-heels dive with an English pub-sounding name, a centuries-old history of serving pints and shots to late-night hangers-on like myself.

Your fellow beings. On the losing side of a dream.

They can change. We *can* change.

That guy at the end of the bar, barely standing, still trying to get the woman on the next stool to come home with him. Look at her. She tries to stand but can't. His place or hers? What could they do if they get there?

I felt myself running out of arguments.

Or those two guys passed out on that bench by the restrooms. Friends? Strangers? Lovers? What does it matter in the land of oblivion?

I surveyed the others along the bar. Hunched like jealous lovers over their drinks. Faces turned inward. Unalterable as a row of tombstones.

I emptied my glass, stared into the room's smoky blue light looking for—*what*? A kindred soul among the damned?

Here I was, beating myself up again. A habit I fell into too easily.

Too late for talk, or reason. Even the jukebox had quit.

Beside the cash register, a portable radio—barely audible—was broadcasting a late-night caller's soulful monologue on the Nite Hawk show. The man was agreeing with the old cliché that women got prettier at closing time. It wasn't so much that, I thought, as one's apartment felt emptier.

The barkeep shouted now from the end of the bar, "Last call."

A too familiar phrase since Vera walked out of my life.

5

On the way back to my apartment, shadows cast upon shadows. The normally inviting brownstones and tree-lined streets appeared cold and alien—dismal, menacing—but the fear they generated had nothing to do with muggers. Its origins were more obscure, having to do with things beyond reach: uncertainties, insecurities, a recognition of my own fragile standing in this world.

Never had I held myself in high regard, but night undermined what little confidence I'd managed to salvage from the wreckage.

Who was I?

A blind man.

A *self*-blinded man. Without tangible foundation for what I was living for, or what animal energy drove me from bed to begin each day.

At my desk I tried to get back to my writing—the story of a man, akin to a character from Kafka's *The Trial*, up against forces he didn't understand, a mystery revealed only in fragments, never in its entirety—but the actual mystery of Vera's disappearance kept intruding, Davison's question hanging unanswered: *What if someone's trying to hurt her, right now?* Then it was his accusatory claim that strong-armed me. You're the key.

Finally I gave up and pushed the typewriter aside. Sitting in the dark, staring at the molding that broke the monotony of the room's white plaster. Listening to the garbage trucks grinding their way between Cherry Lane and Hudson Street.

Sometimes, as I did now, I thought of myself as one of my own characters negotiating an underworld of darkness and confusion, where only a murky line divided good from evil. I was one of the guilty, I was sure of that. Davison had shown up to remind me. His awful words, *She never stopped loving you*, hurled like a curse.

Or maybe, I tried to convince myself, none of this had happened. The night's events only a story I'd conjured. Another fiction among the hundreds I'd invented over the years: strange and mysterious images from some private hell, disembodied voices haunted by fear, anxiety and desire. I'd wake up tomorrow and all this would be gone. I'd spend the night with Connie making love, or trying to, and things would be as they were.

At this hour of night, who could tell what was real, what was dream, hallucination, fantasy, the product of a fevered imagination?

Or was it truth disguised in one or more of those forms?

I didn't expect to find an answer.

Answers, I knew, manifest themselves in daylight. Only to be subverted in these hours in the dark.

6

Vera said, "I've never come before."

Her face, mostly in darkness.

Streetlight filtering through the leaves of the beech tree scattered the bed with shadows. Somewhere in the courtyard a baby was crying, but babies were the last thing we were thinking of.

She was propped on one arm, turned on her side, leaning toward me. Her hair, dark, cut short. Its boyish wave falling forward, always, over one eye. I brushed it back, held it in place—what had become an intimate gesture after love.

"Yes," I said.

"You knew?"

"Yes."

"With anyone," she said. "Not just with you."

That I didn't know. Though I'd wondered.

"Those other times. I really enjoyed them, too." She said it softly. An apology. "In a different way."

"Which made it hard to tell sometimes."

She studied me, estimating—*what*? "How was it different? This time."

I laughed. "You tell *me*."

"You first."

A game we played. Confessional.

"All right."

Her eyes. Clear, dark. Alive with fierce, inquisitive energy visible even in the shadowed light.

"Your body gets tight. In the past, I mean. When you get close. Your hands become fists. Your arms, your shoulders go rigid. Like you're defending yourself, fighting to save your life. This time—" I didn't know how much she wanted to hear.

"This time, what?"

"It was—different."

"Tell me."

"Your hands opened—"

"And?"

"The tension drained from your face and your neck, your arms. It turned into something else. You—" What was the right word? "*Trembled.* In a way I hadn't felt before."

Gone was the curiosity in her eyes, replaced by the softer look of hurt. "Like you were watching me in a movie. Making fun of me."

"I wasn't making fun."

"How could you be that detached?"

"I wasn't detached." I waited before adding: "You know that."

"No. You weren't." She lay back beside me. A sigh I couldn't read. Concession, maybe. Submission.

"Your turn."

"I can't. I'm too embarrassed."

She turned toward the wall. I reached to bring her back.

Her eyes stared past me at the ceiling. "I'm being a baby, aren't I?"

"You haven't finished the game."

"Is the game what matters?"

"Fair is fair." A vow we'd taken from the beginning. What one of us revealed, the other had to reveal in kind. A secret for a secret.

She looked at me directly then, no evasion. It took several moments but, when she spoke, the words came fast. "It felt like this huge wall was crumbling, all around me, and I was terrified. I was going to get hurt, really bad. Then I was part of the wall. But it wasn't pain I was feeling. It was something else. All these colors—blues and pinks and yellows—like flowers with petals softer than the softest velvet, blooming and blooming inside me."

"It was worth the wait, I take it."

She pushed me away and slipped out of bed. Her thin elegant form—narrow-waisted, long-legged—moved with an easy grace to the window.

A shadow.

A silhouette.

A stranger, still.

I joined her there, the two of us staring down at the courtyard's grass and flowers, the baby no longer crying.

I pulled her close.

Another bond, deeper than those that had come before, had been formed between us. I thought: this would keep us together forever.

Despite her marriage, her husband.

Despite the ways our hearts would conspire against us.

Afterward we walked to Hudson Street. A new kind of silence between us. No apology, no awkwardness. A shared thing holding us close.

A cab took her from me.

I watched the car merge into traffic as it moved toward Eighth, following the taillights until I could no longer differentiate them from the other cabs on their flow north.

A habit I'd gotten into: paying close attention to her comings and goings.

Waiting at my window—always early—watching the mouth of the alley for the moment she would emerge into the courtyard. Or standing at an entrance to the park, waiting for her to turn a corner and come into view.

Goodbyes, the hardest. Witnessing her disappearance down the steps of the subway or, like that night, beyond the closed door of a cab. Leaving a ghost of herself behind.

Returning to the apartment, I stood at the window. As if, contrary to all logic, she might appear again at the mouth of the alley as she had earlier that night.

As she had a month before. That very first time.

7

She liked my apartment, she said.

A grey afternoon, early spring.

She liked the way such a dreary alley opened into the unexpected courtyard with its beech tree, its patches of grass and flowers. She liked that all the windows had shutters.

"It's only a studio."

"But a large one," she said.

"It's quiet, at least. Away from the street."

"Hidden away." She seemed to relish that.

She nodded approvingly and moved from the window, ran her hand along the rim of the desk, taking in the room as a whole: the galley kitchen, the door to the bathroom, the bedroom area beyond that. "A sanctuary," she said.

Her eyes lingered on the bed.

But it wasn't the bed that day. We took a cab uptown.

In the park the grey sky turning greyer. Drops of rain, wind-blown, here and there. A wooded path north of the Ramble. Arm in arm, no particular destination. Thunderclaps from a darkening sky. Silvered light in flashes.

Around us other park-goers hurried for the exits. *Our* path coiling deeper into the woods.

A stone tunnel was our shelter.

No surprise, no hesitancy. Only briefly and at great distance did I hear the warning to myself: *She's married. You're crossing a line. You're an interloper*.

Some things are pre-ordained. Her arms were tight around me, her lips on mine. Some things you can't run from.

When the heavy rain came, we were locked against the tunnel's stone. Damp rock against my knuckles. In my hands the soft flesh of her waist, her hips. Warm breath on my neck.

Mist cloaked the dim passageway in a fairytale light.

Outside, worlds away, rain pommeled the walkway.

Thunder bursts, sudden, startling. Wind thrashing the trees.

If I hadn't known before, I knew then.

A door locked into place, shutting away the life I'd known.

No matter the consequences.

I was too deep in love to turn back.

8

Memory drives our future.

In those sleepless hours before dawn, a time between time, I'd made the decision to help find her. Remembering her was like relapsing into an addiction I couldn't control.

As I walked up the driveway, Davison waved to me from their sagging front porch.

Their house sat on a street in Riverdale that eventually wound its way down to the Hudson, though you couldn't see it from their property. Wrong angle, too many trees. An elegant but weather-beaten farmhouse from Colonial times. Way beyond an associate professor's salary.

"Norm's parents," Vera had explained the first time she invited me there. "They gave it to him when they moved to Vermont full-time."

"A life of privilege." An offhand, pointless remark. It wasn't Davison's house I was jealous of.

"Not really," Vera said.

I didn't ask her what she meant.

Now I told myself it was the possibility that she was in danger that brought me back here. Those predictable scenarios of abduction, torture, rape and murder. That played into it, to be sure; there was a sliver of a hero still left in me.

Equally true, though, was this: If she wasn't in danger, if she'd left Davison on her own . . . I was too weak to resist the chance she might come back into my life. And I was angry. Above all I wanted to know, *had* to know, this: if life hadn't turned out the way she wanted, if Davison was right in saying she never stopped loving me, why hadn't she contacted me? No husband, no child now stood in the way. All of which left me baffled, and worse.

It was my turn to feel humiliated.

9

That first time here, years before, Vera and I hadn't yet made love.

Still, I was trespassing. I knew that.

She introduced me as "that writer I met at the soup kitchen," a phrase that though true to the facts seemed insufficient. Someone once wrote about the art of poetry that what is left out is as important, maybe more important, than what is left in. I thought of that then, smiling dumbly to mask my uneasiness, thrusting out my hand to shake Davison's.

He'd just won some academic prize for his work on the mating habits of orangutans so he was pretty full of himself. In fact he'd bought himself a pair of dress boots—a creamy brown in color, Italian leather, expensive as hell by the looks of them—to celebrate.

Cocktails in the beamed-ceiling living room, Davison opening the box and pulling on his boots, parading before their nineteenth-century fireplace to show them off, this newfound proof he'd transformed from stuffy professor to hipster. The self-congratulatory tone of it turned me off. Only later, after Vera and I were lovers, did I look back on his behavior that night with a kind of sadness.

Dinner was T-bone steak topped with mushrooms, fried potatoes, a tomato and onion salad. The only meal, Vera confessed, she felt confident enough to serve to guests. "So you'll be having this every time you come over," she warned me. A smile both warm and coy, a smile of intimations.

"Absolutely," Davison added, "I hope we'll be seeing a lot more of you." Though as it turned out that was the first and only meal the three of us shared.

Dinner conversation: friendly, polite, bland.

I asked him about the prize he won.

"Nothing really," he said.

"It's only the most prestigious award the Association gives," Vera said, giving his hand a squeeze.

His face flushed. "Now, now, dear."

"What exactly are the essentials of the orangutan love life?" I asked.

"Well, it's precisely how similar they are to our own."

He talked on about their mating habits, their constancy in love, their devotion to the family structure. I couldn't help but thinking all well and good but wouldn't it make more sense to study human sexual mores directly. Wouldn't that teach us all we needed to know about our possibilities and limitations, our against-all-odds successes, our sordid failures?

He asked me about my book that had just come out. My first—the one that earned me barely enough to put a down payment on my apartment. It seemed, though, he was only being the consummate host, that he knew little of and had little interest in the writer's world.

He shifted the conversation to the soup kitchen, how grateful he was Vera had taken an interest in volunteering there, how it gave her some focus at this point in her life when she was still figuring out what she wanted to do. He gave her an indulgent smile. It seemed intended to remind her how fortunate she was that she had the luxury—all the time in the world really—to find herself. A luxury most women her age, for she had just turned 28, wouldn't have.

The insinuation seemed clear: certainly not one married to a financially insecure fledgling novelist.

Or was I pushing that too far? Self-doubt, my eternal sidekick.

"You'll have to invite us down to see this new pad of yours in the Village. That is, if Vera hasn't had a chance to see it yet."

"No, no, I haven't," she was quick to say.

"Of course," I said. "I'd love to have you both down. Whenever you'd like."

He smiled at Vera benevolently. Then turned to me, shaking my hand as he excused himself. "Early classes tomorrow. Some material to read over. I'll leave you in the capable hands of my lovely wife."

His step on the stairs, then crossing the room above us.

At the table there were empty plates and bunched napkins between us. "Time to go," I said.

"You don't have to. Not yet."

The temptation to stay was strong, but I hadn't yet abandoned my scruples. I hadn't yet lost the power to make rational decisions.

In the mud room before I pulled open the door, there was a moment we stood close.

Shyness in her smile. "I'm glad you came over."

"I'm glad, too."

"Monday," she called after me as I went down the driveway. The night we volunteered. Serving dinner to the homeless.

She made it sound like a promise.

10

Davison reached to shake my hand. "So glad you're here. I was afraid I'd laid too heavy a burden on you last night." Self-consciously, he pushed open the door and waited for me to enter.

I hesitated.

"It's all right," he assured me. Then he was beside me, ushering me into the room and the door slammed shut behind us with a thud of finality.

For a moment it occurred to me this might be a trap, that it had taken this long, a decade, for him to enact his revenge. First he'd murdered Vera; now it was my turn.

But this wasn't one of my novels.

Davison was deep in thought. "I know how odd this must be for you. After what happened. But let's forget about that, shall we? That's in the past. We have a common purpose now."

Forgetting the past? How was that possible?

He observed me in an easy, straightforward way. The man's equanimity, the calm he maintained under duress, impressed me as it had back then. He smiled like the host he had been the night I came to dinner. Frankly, I didn't know how he could do it. For my part, it was impossible to ignore the pounding in my chest. I moved a step away from him.

"I thought you might find something here to help in our search, something I might have missed." He took in the room with a sense of pride. "Vera's made it a lot cozier since you last saw it."

Cozy wasn't the word I would have chosen.

Crammed with a mishmash of antique and contemporary furnishings, the living room had been completely made over. Knickknacks everywhere. On shelves and table tops and cupboards. Hummels, ceramic objects, glass figurines.

"Vera loved these—these mementoes," Davison said. "She had to have a souvenir from every place we went." He held up a figure of a bear on skis, the bear's right paw raised in a wave. "This from an inn in Williamstown that she liked. We'd drive up there sometimes on a Sunday afternoon in winter, if she was feeling bored or restless."

Animal figurines overwhelmed the shelves. Turtles, dogs, deer, rabbits, an elephant, a rhino, even a unicorn or two. Despite Davison's insistence that Vera still loved me, I couldn't help but see—irrational as it was—in every figurine she had amassed, every piece of furniture and every collectible, another in an interminable series of betrayals. The life she'd chosen without me.

The walls of the room were heavily adorned, as well: paintings, tapestries, framed photographs, posters. As if empty space were her mortal enemy. She had to destroy it wherever it exposed itself.

It was the oddest of situations, trying to find the woman I knew in the cluttered assortment of detail. When I first saw this room, her tastes in interior design had run to the opposite extreme. She was a minimalist: mostly bare white walls with an occasional piece of teak furniture. A reaction, she said, to her mother and her grandmother's heavy mahogany pieces and thick floral drapes, what she referred to as the "suffocation style" of home furnishing.

It took a moment before I found something familiar. A poster from a Cezanne exhibit at the Met, the Impressionists an inspiration of hers. Rainy Sunday afternoons, if Davison was busy, we visited the museum's permanent collection. Impressionism was created for rainy Sunday afternoons, she would insist. I would have preferred us to stay dry in the comfort of my apartment.

On a table, far corner of the room, a framed photograph of her: her hair longer, below her neck; her lips pursed in an unfamiliar way. But the real changes were more subtle. It wasn't that her eyes and her smile were less radiant so much as the radiance seemed forced, as if she'd strained to re-invigorate it for the purpose of the photo.

Upstairs, I followed him down a short hall. Past the guest room which I knew all too well, my heart pounding again. The double bed with its embroidered coverlet. The broad branches of an ancient tree beyond the windows. The smell of pine on a summer night.

The door to the master bedroom was closed. Davison opened it and stepped inside, waiting for me. Again I hesitated. The last thing I wanted to see was the mattress upon which they'd made love, conceived their child. And wasn't it all too bizarre, exposing me to the intimacies of their private life? Another indication of how desperate he was?

"Are you all right?" Davison asked.

I nodded, without looking at him. I stepped inside, gave the room a cursory look: the closet with its half-opened door, a pair of jeans and a T-shirt thrown in one corner. A woman's shoe on the floor nearby. A dress thrown over the back of a chair.

It was an oppressive room, or so it seemed to me. The air thick and close, smelling faintly of something floral. The scent came from an open perfume bottle on the vanity. A sign of her forgetfulness? Had she been in a hurry to get somewhere?

I forced myself to confront the bed. The coverlet on one side had been neatly drawn, left undisturbed. A nearby window offered late morning light.

"It must be strange for you," he said.

Strange too simple and weak a word for what I felt: displaced, disordered. Anger rising like a chokehold on my throat.

"You sure I can't get you something? Water? A whiskey?"

"I'm fine." I wondered if he appreciated the glaring irony: him offering *me* comfort. Though maybe that irony missed the point. After all, in the end, it was he who had bested me.

If I were a detective in one of my novels, I would have conducted a closer inspection of the room. But I was too distressed to linger. Maybe another time.

Downstairs in the kitchen, I concentrated on more transparent things. It was cleaner, better organized than I remembered.

In those days her housekeeping rule had been a simple one: bathroom had to be fastidiously clean, everything else could go to hell. In the center of the room, a relic from the 50s, a small Formica dinette set with chrome legs where she'd served me coffee.

A baby's cup sat on an open shelf, the name *Devon* spelled out in red lettering in the shape of flowers.

Their child, he'd told me, had died only a year before. The boy was nine at the time. Yet this, I realized, was the only evidence I'd come across that Devon had ever existed.

11

Down a narrow flight of stairs. A windowless basement smelling of dampness and must. Vera's studio.

Beneath ceiling pipes, two wooden work tables laden with black & white photos. A loop of wire holding a row of photos attached via clothespins.

Images with piercing clarity, unique angles, a singular focus.

A man and a woman in shadow, their embrace so close impossible to tell where one body began and the other ended.

A man's hand raised to touch a woman's cheek.

A teenage boy and girl kissing, silhouetted against what appeared to be a subway tunnel.

"The night she disappeared," Davison said. "She'd gone to the park with her camera. Her therapy, she began calling it, after Devon died."

"Do you mind my asking what your son died of?"

Davison looked surprised by the question. "Simply put, his heart gave out. You knew he had Down Syndrome, didn't you?"

"I didn't."

"I'm sorry. I assumed, I don't know why, that you did."

"No."

He looked at me closely. "I know what you're thinking. Not to worry, though. It's not what you would imagine. When Devon was born the way he was, I was afraid she'd go into some deep depression. But she didn't. Not at all. She loved that kid like he was the most beautiful child ever conceived. Strapped him to her in this papoose-like contraption. Took him everywhere."

He leaned against the workbench, watching me. "I tried to warn her about getting too attached, that the prognosis wasn't good. Not only did he have a weak heart, some of his other organs were compromised, as well. But she couldn't help herself. When he died, a year ago this month, she fell apart—"

He cupped his hand over his eyes, not finishing his thought. When he dropped his hand, he looked at me in apology. "This is all still hard for me to process." He took a deep breath before going on: "She started drinking, and whatever. She wandered through the house like an abandoned child. It wasn't until she fell one night and broke her collarbone that she agreed to go into rehab. And in time she came out of it, she kicked her addiction, and for a while she seemed happier than I'd seen her in months. She seemed ready to start over."

All these years, in my heart's netherlands, she'd been only a lover to me, an object of desire. *Enshrined* in memory: a romantic fantasy, untouched by time or adversity. I tried not to feel like a fool in light of the pain life had crippled her with.

I turned to the fence of photos hanging from the wire. The lovers. On city streets, in parks. "These are the most recent?"

"She took them the day before she disappeared."

They were gentle in tone, *affectionate*, except for the last two. One showed a woman's frightened face, a man in shadow looming over her, his hand around her pony tail, yanking back her head. The other was equally disturbing. The same two people. The woman on the ground half-undressed, the man on top of her, his hand raised in a fist about to strike.

Had Vera witnessed an assault somewhere in the park? Could this have something to do with the danger she was in?

I asked Davison that.

He seemed flustered and embarrassed, shrugging it off, saying he didn't know how she found her subjects. He took a step to block the two disturbing photos from my view.

"Before she disappeared, had there been any reason to believe she was in danger?"

"Other than what I told you—the phone calls at odd hours, the agitation—no," Davison said. "Everything seemed more or less normal."

"More or less?"

"As I've said, she seemed on edge. I suggested a mini-vacation, that we go away for a weekend somewhere to relax. But she didn't seem to go for that idea."

"Other than that—?"

"Other than that, there was nothing out of the ordinary. Until she didn't come home."

12

Under the heading, *Fears: Both Real and Imagined,* I found this fragment, one of the latest entries in Vera's journal.

Davison had given me the journal before I left, saying, "Under other circumstances I'd consider this a breach of privacy, but that's the least of my worries now. Maybe you can make more sense of it than I did." He held the ringed notebook out tentatively. "Something to help us find her."

There were *two* violations of privacy here: his and *mine*. I felt uneasy about it. But that didn't stop me from reading, huddled at my desk, the last light of day fading from the courtyard.

"The man lives in the shadows. In the corner of a room or on a darkened street or in the shade of trees. It seems sometimes the shadows themselves are the danger. She, poor fool that she is, seeks refuge inside her castle, but the castle itself is no longer safe. There are doors and windows he can break. There are guards he can bribe.

In her dreams she is running. From dungeon to dungeon. Like a primitive cave drawing, the man's silhouette rises in shadow on the walls. His arm is raised. His hand is reaching out for her.

A matter of time.

Everything, especially death, is a matter of time. . . ."

So which was this, I wondered, a fear that was real, or imagined?

What came before it was a random collection of thoughts and observations. And stories about Devon.

Apparently the boy had trouble keeping his balance even when she held his hand for support. *It was like he was on ice,* she wrote. *His feet would fly out from under him like skates on a slippery surface. He would fall but never in the same way. Backwards sometimes. Other times forward. Or to one side or the other. It was the look on his face that broke my heart. Sprawled on the floor like that. The look of stunned and absolute incomprehension. Looking at me as if I'd betrayed him. Making me feel at times even more guilty than I already did. Not only had I created this child whose mental and motor skills were inadequate to negotiate the world, but now it seemed I was powerless to help him succeed in this, the most basic of human endeavors. For the longest time he was unable even to pull himself into a sitting position. Even that was too far beyond his means.*

It took them, she went on to say, with the help of intensive therapies, three and a half years before he could walk relatively comfortably on his own, and even then he moved slowly, nowhere near sure-footed. On the street he wouldn't walk without holding her hand. Norm, she made a point to say, had long since given up in despair. *But Devon never did. His spirit would flame out in his crooked smile and in his eyes with their perpetual upward slant. Which made me love him even more. If that were possible. If it was at all possible that I could love him more than I did.*

In those years before he could walk on his own, she talked of taking him with her whenever she left the house. *I was determined to expose him to the world and to what normal children experienced. In whatever way I could.*

A comment several pages farther along made me stop reading for a moment. In her papoose-carrying days, one of the therapists told her Devon was so developmentally disabled he might never achieve the cognitive ability of even a five year old. *I knew then*, she said, *that he was my baby for as long as he lived. And that God had made him that way to give me a reason to go on.*

This from the woman I knew as carefree, even wildly reckless. Who had never mentioned God in any reverential way, whose only purpose seemed to be to push things, especially our love, to the limit.

I poured myself a whiskey and then another.

There were phone numbers for realty offices in Portland,

Oregon and St. Paul, Minnesota. Descriptions of houses and condos, number of bedrooms and bathrooms, proximity to public transportation, schools, churches.

I called each of the real estate agencies she listed. None were willing to talk about their clients but when I pushed, when I gave them the story of her disappearance, how I was helping her husband track her down, two of them agreed to answer questions. The Kent Agency in Portland said she'd inquired about several rental apartments in the city, that she was hoping to move there by summer's end. Their last correspondence with her had been two weeks ago, on May 25th.

The Miller and Sons Agency of St. Paul said she'd called about an apartment. She had, in fact, been considering making an offer on one particular condo. She was planning a trip, the office manager said, to view the property in person. It had been twelve days, he added, since their last correspondence. Which, I noted, would have been right before she disappeared.

I wondered if the two different locations were a smoke-screen she was using to cover her tracks. Or was it the kind of grass-is-always-greener fantasy-dream we all indulge in?

What if . . . ?

Mine came typically in winter. The dull wind-bitten days of January and February when the city shivered and Florida beckoned in the guise of a tropical paradise rather than the way I'd heard it once described—perhaps more accurately—as an exit ramp for the old and infirm.

I turned the page and there appeared what seemed to be a random question scribbled on the top line: *What is the beauty of the Blue Flower?*

And again, a similar reference farther down on the same page: *The Blue Flower awaits. Do we dare a rendezvous with death*?

Another fear? Real or imagined?

In the cone of light from the desk lamp, I studied the photos Davison had given me. The pulse of yearning and promise, the vulnerability in the eyes of the lovers. The sheer number of images—a hundred and fifty or so by my count—overwhelming in and of itself.

When I'd asked Davison about them, whether he was bothered by her pre-occupation with the subject matter, he had shrugged and said, "I'm a scientist, she's an artist. All artists have a particular subject matter, don't they? Gauguin had his Tahitian women, Dali had his crucifixions, the Impressionists their gardens."

Yes, but still—I'd wanted to say.

Love, *young* love. Sweet and tender.

The two violent, erotically charged photos—the dream turned nightmare—that had been hanging in the basement were missing.

I wasn't sure what to make of that.

13

3 a.m.

I closed the journal, pushed aside the photos, poured another whiskey. On the radio, Nite Hawk's voice broke the silence of the room:

What do we do with the night?

We sleep.

We dream.

We fall, then fall deeper . . .

This night's story was from a cab driver in lower Manhattan, telling of his most unusual fare, "a real skinny guy in a black raincoat" who at midnight would wait for him on the corner of Delancey and Suffolk, tell him to simply drive around, no particular destination. After an hour or two, the man would tip him a hundred bucks or so and tell him to pick him up the next night, same time, same place. Turns out, the man had some kind of cancer, couldn't stand spending the long night hours alone in his apartment. So these nightly rides went on for a week straight. On the eighth night the man showed up with a satchel, said it was for his girlfriend in Brooklyn. She'd recently dumped him but they'd had some good times together and he wanted to give her something, kind of a farewell gift. On the way to Brooklyn, the man wanted to stop a minute on the Manhattan Bridge, to take a picture of the skyline. "Normally," the cabbie said, "I'd never do a thing like that, no way, but it was late, a Sunday night, no traffic to speak of, and besides the guy had been damn good to me. Next thing I know he's outta the cab, he's climbing the guard rail and, like that, he drops outta sight. When I get to the rail I don't see nothin', just grey water down below, heaving this way and that. So I pull off the bridge, call 9-1-1. That's when I notice the satchel in the back seat. Turns out, it's jam packed with bills. No I.D., no nothin'. Just fifteen thousand bucks when I count it later.

I put it in the trunk, say nothin' to the cops. When they fish the guy out the next day, he's got no identification on him, just his skinny body in a raincoat. That was over a year ago. The money's still in the satchel. The satchel's under my bed. I take it out sometimes just to look. Haven't spent a dime of it. Not a dime." He waited before adding: "Stories without an end. They're the ones you never forget."

"That's our allotment of heartfelt illumination for this night," Nite Hawk's voice said to conclude the broadcast, a voice so bold and rich and god-like I didn't know if it was a reassurance in the lonely hours or an evocation of the depthless dark of the cosmos.

What do we do with the night?

We sleep.

We dream.

We wander, wonder. What is real, what is not?

Downstairs in the courtyard I lit a cigarette. I'd taken up my old habit again, buying a pack of Luckies after coming back from Davison's. For years after Vera left, I measured my nights in whiskies and smokes and the number of pages I managed to get written. Desperation's closest friends.

In time, though, coffee replaced the booze and I gave up nicotine; the pages, the endless pages got me through. So this, I told myself, this embrace of old comforts, was only temporary. Nothing permanent. Only long enough to survive this rough patch.

In the shadow of the beech tree, I tried to find my usual comfort in the courtyard fountain. The figure of a frolicking Cupid. The water's steady and eternal splash and drip. The solace of that.

No lights in the surrounding apartments. Even the garbage trucks had made their final rounds. A rare moment of urban calm.

I drew again on the cigarette, holding the smoke deep inside, in search of whatever ersatz satisfaction it might yield. Something, but not enough. I flicked away the cigarette and crumpled the pack of Luckies, dropping it in a trash bin.

Then I was thinking again about Vera, her life without me: the house she shared with Davison, their lost child, her disappearance. And the endless photos—with god knows what buried intentions—she'd left behind.

Anonymous couples in love that now, like so many regrets, lay scattered across my desk.

Stories without an end.

14

Where does a love affair begin? The *true* beginning.

Is it an incident in childhood? Some trivial thing perhaps, or something more consequential that sets off a concatenation of infinitesimal adjustments to our personality pre-disposing us to be receptive to a certain man, a certain woman. What obscure journeys of the mind and heart had I travelled all my years to bring me to Vera that Monday night, ten years past?

The Church of the Apostles. Upper East Side.

Several hundred homeless people assembled for their weekly sit-down dinner. The church basement fancied up with red streamers. A red crepe-paper WELCOME sign sagging unevenly on the back wall.

I'd been volunteering most of the winter and spring. I liked to think it was the altruistic part of my nature that brought me there. Which, I believe now, was partly true. The other part was need. Apart from my writing, not much happening in my life—loner that I was. Nights, even then, something to endure. The basement, by contrast, bright with light, the chatter of voices, the bustle of waiters like myself bringing plates of hot food from the serving line to our respective tables. A party for the down-and-out, but a party nonetheless.

I was manning the coffee/tea/soft drinks counter. Vera, a woman I hadn't yet met, serving tables on the room's far side.

Rasmus, an elderly bearded homeless man who left the 'E' off his formal name, held an empty to-go coffee cup out to me.

I took it from his shaking hand. "Cream?"

"Nope."

"Sugar?"

"Yup."

I tipped the sugar dispenser, stopped at what I thought

was a generous two teaspoonsful.

"More," he said.

I tipped the dispenser again.

"Keep goin'," he said. "I'll tell you when. Keep goin'. Keep goin'. That's right. Keep goin'."

At three-quarters full, he said, "That be good. That be good."

I filled what little space remained in the cup with an ounce or two of coffee.

"High octane," he said by way of explanation before taking the cup and turning away. "Gotta rev them engines. Gotta get where I'm goin'."

"Where's that?" a woman said beside me. "The moon?"

Somehow the old man despite being hard of hearing and already several feet away, caught what she said. "No, ma'am," he said with a solemn, deadly serious face. "Uptown. One thirty-fifth and Lex."

The woman's face colored with embarrassment. "I'm sorry," she said. "I didn't mean to—" Quickly she took an empty cup from the counter, filling it three-quarters with sugar and adding a dollop of coffee. She held it out to him. "In case you need—in case the one you have's not enough."

The old man bowed his grizzled head in gratitude. "Bless you, woman. God be sure to bless you."

The woman, still embarrassed, looked at me sheepishly. "My daddy always warned me my smart mouth would get me in trouble."

Then she held out her hand. "I'm Vera," she said.

15

Love's a matter of sexual timing, Gertrude Stein once said.

That's part of it, I'm sure.

But I'd known attractive women before. So sexuality alone didn't account for my feelings for Vera.

I liked the way she found a benign amusement in those we served. Volunteering at the church, for me, had been a matter of a singular narrow focus, the serious business of helping the needy. Ladling soup into a bowl carefully to avoid spillage, bringing extra bread or crackers or packets of salt or sugar to those who requested them, making sure the entrée was served hot, that everyone got a salad and dessert. Vera lightened the mood. She performed her duties *and* took pleasure in the night's oddities. Like the woman who, at the end of each meal, would tell us in all seriousness that the service here was terrible, she wouldn't be caught dead eating in this second-rate establishment again, only to be the first one seated at our table the following week.

And the man Vera called Mr. GQ who wore the scruffiest, dirtiest clothes and shoes imaginable, except for his leather jacket which looked as if it might have sold at Bloomingdale's or Saks for a thousand dollars or more. And there was Dr. Minestrone (Vera's name for him), the soup man. A middle-aged, Sicilian gentleman who ate nothing but soup. Always asking for seconds or thirds. If we ran out, he'd sit there stone-faced and sullen the rest of the meal, ignoring the food that was put before him. At meal's end he would go from table to table, in search of bowls of unfinished soup which he'd pour into three thermos jugs he carried in his knapsack. And the man who would often sit next to him who wouldn't touch the soup at all, who only wanted the round little oyster crackers that came with it. One at a time he'd place them on his tongue and let them melt there like a communion wafer. He and Dr. Minestrone man became fast friends, at least for the length of the meal.

And the black man who hit on whatever white waitress served his food, promising them a night on the town and, to begin the evening, champagne cocktails at his place. "Oh my," Vera said to me, rolling her eyes, after the sixth or seventh time he made his pitch to her. "Every woman's dream. Champagne cocktails under a bridge. Or, better yet, in a subway tunnel. Hope truly doth spring eternal."

This was her way—she told me the second night we worked together—meaning the quips and asides she shared with me, of keeping herself from getting depressed at the lives of these lonely, forsaken people.

While we stood around waiting for them to finish their meal, she would try to imagine where they spent the night after they left the safety of the church basement. Riding the subways to keep warm, or on a park bench, or huddled against the side of a building or wrapped in cardboard in a doorway or on the steps of a church. She tried to match what she could see of their personality with the type of makeshift dwelling they might inhabit. "He's definitely a subway tunnel kind of guy," or "she's a bench lady, probably lower level Grand Central," or "he's the kind of guy you see wrapped in a blanket on the sidewalk outside Port Authority." But what really concerned her—it was close to an obsession, I'd say—was how they fell from grace.

By their own hand?

By the hand of destiny?

One particular woman, Miriam, fascinated her more than the others. A thin, elegant white-haired woman who always wore a dress. Her hair and face perfectly made up. During dinner she rarely spoke to anyone; rather, she sat primly and read a book. Usually a classic novel from the eighteenth or nineteenth century. Edith Wharton or Jane Austen or Emily Bronte. A different one each week.

Vera would stand off to the side and study her: the regal

lines of her face, her high cheekbones, delicate nose, rounded chin; the careful way she held her fork, cut her meat, dabbed her mouth with a napkin. Whenever she tried to engage the woman in conversation, Miriam was always polite, offering a gracious smile but little else.

"What happened?" Vera asked me one night.

"Why is she homeless? Is that what you're asking?"

"She's obviously well-bred, educated, likely from money. She doesn't seem mentally ill like some of the others."

"Bad luck, I guess."

"What *kind* of bad luck, though?"

I offered the usual kind of reasons: loss of a job, a personal catastrophe, a drinking or a drug problem, an emotional breakdown of some sort.

"Hope," Vera said.

"What about it?"

"I think she lost hope. She had a good life, all the amenities, all the blessings, but she began to lose things, one after the other: a child maybe, a close friend, a husband, a house. Each loss stealing another piece of her will until she didn't care anymore and she just gave up."

"Except for her appearance," I said. "She obviously still cares about that."

Vera stared past me, her dark curious eyes watching Miriam at the table, book in hand as she waited for the main course to be served—that night, chicken with rice and mixed vegetables.

"It's a thin line, isn't it," Vera said, "between hope and despair."

16

Women, lost or adrift. An attraction of mine.

Those whose lives were still unformed. Who hadn't yet found, within themselves and in the world, what they were looking for. Women as lost as myself.

After college, Vera told me, she'd gone from job to job: receptionist at a museum, substitute teacher in a high school, secretary at a law firm. Nothing that held her interest. Nothing she stayed with very long. She'd double-majored in art and English and didn't know which of them to commit to. She wasn't sure she wanted a career or motherhood, or both.

When we met she'd begun dabbling in photography, taking a class here and there at the New School. "I can't always find the words, but I can always find a picture that says what I want to say," she told me one Monday night at a bar near the church. An Irish pub we'd spend time in after serving dinner.

She shrugged when she said it, something helpless in her look. "Kind of like driving blind into a storm. That's been my life. Then I met Norm. He was already established. Stable, secure. An anchor. A young girl's dream."

She smiled at that but I was seeing something beneath the smile. Maybe it was the phrase, *Or so I thought*, omitted at the end of her last sentence. A woman on unsteady ground, a woman adrift. Which always bolstered my confidence. I had something to offer, some manner of help to guide her through troubled waters, though it would take years before I realized it was myself I was ultimately trying to help.

How easily our priorities shift.

It wasn't helping the needy I looked forward to on Monday nights, as much as this hour or two we spent in a dark corner of that Irish pub.

God, in whom she told me she'd stopped believing about

the time she lost her virginity, was a topic she liked to pounce on like a cat going after a bird. “Don’t you think it odd,” she asked, “that an omnipotent, all-knowing and all-powerful being, would give a damn whether or not anyone worshipped him or not? I mean, this guy controls everything in the universe, why does he need praise from lowly creatures like ourselves?”

She rolled the rim of the beer glass across her lips, a habit of hers when she was thinking something through. She set the glass down without drinking. Rarely did she finish even the one glass per night she ordered. “One more pitiful example,” she said, “of man creating God in his own image. *We’re* the ones in need, not some abstract almighty ruler of the world.”

I said I thought churches with their doctrines and dogma were an impediment to, rather than a facilitator of, grace. “True grace,” I said a bit too pompously, “comes from acts of human charity.”

On this, we agreed. Though she did say she had at least some respect for the Church of the Apostles. “They don’t let the god thing stand in the way of using their basement for something practical.”

Another Monday night at the pub.

Our hour together each week growing longer. On the jukebox, an old standard from the 30s. *I’ll Be Seeing You.*

In one of those tiny and almost impossibly coincidental connections that bring us together as couples, both *her* father and mine had loved that song. “He used to sing it to me whenever one of us was sad or unhappy,” she told me. “His lullaby for the waking hours.” My father, by contrast, would sing it whenever *he* was *particularly* happy, when he was in sync with the world, when he thought things were going his way.

It became the way Vera and I ended our nights. *I’ll be seeing you.* A wish. A hope. A promise.

And later, after we became lovers, on those days we stole more time for each other, she would insist we find *our* special places. Our small café, which was of course our Irish pub. Our wishing well, which was Cupid’s fountain in my courtyard. Our favorite tree—not a chestnut tree but the beech tree whose leaves we could see from my bed. Our children's carousel was the one in the park, near Sheep Meadow.

But that Monday night we first heard the song together she said simply that all good friends had their special places, places they would always share, that were theirs alone. "They store them in their hearts," she said, "which is the museum of all things loved and cherished, lost or abandoned, which is everywhere, which is the world."

Despite her claim of inadequacy at finding the right words for things, of how much more adept she was with pictures than with language, she was a master of poetic insight and the unique ways she found to express that insight.

It was almost midnight, the latest night we'd shared.

The jukebox had quit.

Silence falling between us.

The future holding its breath.

Her eyes were hard to read. Their darkness a mask. They brushed mine only briefly, before looking downward at the table.

She had such small, slender wrists. Holding a beer glass, or lying flat on the table as they were then, hands crossed. What weight could they bear?

The silence, those fragile and delicate wrists, carrying me to a long-sought serenity beyond that place, that moment.

17

A rainy Sunday. A Monet exhibit at the Met.

The rain always disturbed her, she said, set her on edge. She'd read somewhere that rain was the sound of the soul weeping. "Guess I don't want to hear what my soul has to cry about," she said, and laughed. "Kind of like the heart. I want to know it's beating, but I don't want to *feel* it beating because then—what?—then I couldn't ignore how fragile it is, or how precarious *life* is."

"Maybe if you knew the cause of the weeping you could address it." The logical side of me speaking.

"Oh, that would be too exhausting," she said with the short, bright laugh she used to dismiss what she didn't want to deal with. "Besides, some mysteries can't be solved. *You* should know that as a writer, a *mystery* writer."

I reminded her that she didn't seem to mind the thunderstorm, that first time we made love in the park tunnel.

"Oh, but that was different. *That* was exciting. It's the steady, drip-drip-drip kind that gets to me. You know, the all day rain. The kind you think is never going to end." Then, because she thought she was being too morbid, she laughed it away. "There's a Upanishad legend that claims the spirits of the dead reside on the moon, and return to earth in the falling rain. Probably that's what it is. All those dead spirits harassing the hell out of me."

Norm was busy that Sunday, some article he was writing for a prestigious journal. So she had turned to me. Under the arched entrance to the museum, we watched the rain run in tiny rivulets down the long set of steps, pooling in the gutters of the avenue, as she told me of her rainy-day blues. "Sunday afternoon rains are the worst," she said. "So many quiet hours to get through."

Inside we strolled through the exhibit. Vera lingering over each painting as if it might be the last time she would ever see it. She was fascinated by the series of water lilies paintings, how Monet focused intensively on a particular subject, returning to it again and again, creating different emotional effects by changing color, angle, light, the distance at which we viewed it. "It's like he was seeing the entire world through the prism of those lilies," she said.

"We all have our obsessions," I said. In a time I couldn't yet have imagined, I would think of her endless photos of lovers as an extension of *her* obsessions.

That Sunday, though, in her early days as a photographer, her interest was in landscapes not people. So she reveled in Monet's renderings of the artist's gardens, a spring field, the beautiful *Lilies of the Sun*. That day it was another artist, Edvard Munch, she quoted: *Nature is not something that can be seen by the eye alone—it also lies within the soul, in pictures seen by the inner eye.*

"That's what I love about Monet," she said. "His inner eye distorts the objects in his landscape just enough to give it a deeper, more personal meaning and a deeper beauty."

Another Sunday. Rain falling on the steps of the museum. Inside, an Edward Hopper exhibit.

Vera fixated on the stories his paintings told.

A naked woman half in shadow, half in light, standing alone in a room, looking out a window as morning arrives in a city. What does she see? What does she feel?

A woman stares from a house at an empty field.

A woman alone at a table in an automat looks forlornly down at her coffee cup, black night filling the window behind her.

"His women are so alienated, so—abandoned," she said. "What are they longing for?"

"What do *you* think?"

For a moment her face seemed as vacant as the faces of the women in the paintings. "I don't know. I don't think *they* know. That's what makes his work so unsettling."

The last painting in the exhibit, one titled *Western Motel*, showed a woman sitting alone on a bed, suitcases packed. She's turned away from the window, looking into the room which may or may not be empty. Behind her, out the window, can be seen the partial hood of a parked Buick and an empty road beyond that, and beyond the road a series of darkly ominous hills.

As in Hopper's other paintings, the woman's expression is difficult to decipher. Her face a blank enough mask to hide any number of possibilities.

"She's waiting for someone," Vera theorized. "Is he in the room or outside in the Buick? Is he a stranger or someone she knows? Have they just arrived or are they about to leave? Is she looking forward to the journey or dreading it? There's tension here, for sure. Something's not right. Hopper casts everything in a mood of suspense." She gave me her bright, inquisitive smile.

I studied the painting a while longer. "You're right about the tension. Maybe a crime was committed, or is about to be."

"Something illegal, or a crime of the heart?"

"Could be either, I guess." I saw crime, any crime, as a moral problem that could only be resolved on a moral level. In my writing the crime was merely a device to get at the workings of the human psyche; it was never an end in itself.

Vera said, shaking her head in regret, "I don't think things are going to end well for this woman."

At the time it seemed like an innocent enough remark. It was only later, after she'd disappeared and I'd begun my search for her, that I came to think her concern for Hopper's alienated women was a reflection of her own concerns about her future.

18

I re-read her journal entry entitled *Fears, Both Real and Imagined.*

I was reminded of a phrase I'd jotted down about her in a notebook those early days of our love: *A nameless dread rode the wings of her moods*. It was a line I thought I might use to describe a character in a novel I was working on. That nameless dread was something I'd sensed in Vera—always fleetingly—gone before I could give it much thought, lost in the headlong rush of our desire. One of those things easier to identify in retrospect.

I wrote that line after we made love on the banks of the Hudson. Down the hill from her house in Riverdale. A night she was full of enthusiasm at first, *insisting* that we do this. It was a special place, she said. One that she'd gone to many times by herself. A place tucked into the trees, hidden from the world. Near the tracks of Metro North. She wanted to share it with me. She wanted me to be a part of it.

Walking along the edge of the tracks, the river on one side, thick trees and brush on the other. Near dark.

"It's all right," she said, "I know the way by heart. Even in the dark." But when darkness fell completely she hesitated. Her step slower, more cautious. At one point she held back, reluctant to cross the tracks.

"What's the matter?"

"A train might come. It's not safe."

"We'll hear it. We'll see it. The whistle, the lights."

"What about the third rail?"

"We'll step over it. We won't get hurt." It was my desire now that carried us forward. "It's going to be okay."

We were searching for a bower formed by three closely-positioned trees—her secret place—between the tracks and the slope of the hill, the two of us stumbling through the dark, Vera clinging to my outstretched hand. The enclosure we eventually found darker than the night. Branch and vine shutting out the lights of ships on the river, shutting out the newly-risen silver moon's glow.

Touch was our only guide.

The hand that beckons. The fingers that stretch and grope and grasp.

In the air, the smell of autumn leaves burning.

From far off, a ship's horn.

My hands found the rough edge of her coat, then the softness of hips and thighs, the reaching. For a moment again, her hesitancy. Uncertainty, not desire, in the way she held me.

"Tell me everything will be all right."

"Of course it will."

"Promise me."

"I promise."

Promises are such treacherous things.

Why do we make such grandiose ones?

19

Sue Quinn led me into the bar, swinging her hips in a way that called attention to the brevity of her skirt, her compact rear end and slim, elegant legs.

In Vera's wilder, pre-Devon days we'd double-dated a few times. She worked, then as now, for a legendary northern Manhattan banquet and catering place called *The Manor*: a garish spot known for its faux-European excess, as in pink champagne bubbling from fountains and the mouths of mischievous Cupids. Davison told me he'd contacted her, but she hadn't been helpful. My impression was he didn't think much of her; in fact, at one point, he said he often thought she was a bad influence on Vera. When I asked him why, he said she was "a bit too wild, too unconventional, for his taste. A free spirit," he said, but it was clearly not a compliment.

On the phone Sue seemed caught off-guard. "You're not calling to plan a wedding, I hope."

"Not hardly."

"Good. That would be way out-of-character for a man like you." Her laugh came with a faint nervous tint. Not something I remembered from when she was Vera's spunky and subversive, devil-may-care sidekick.

When I'd arrived she asked what I thought of their newly re-decorated fifty by twenty-five foot mural of a moonlit bridal couple kissing passionately in a lush garden overflowing with flowers of throbbing color, deep reds and yellows and pinks. Across the top of the mural, encapsulated in an unfurling scroll, were the words: *Let all who pass through here glory in the promise of Eden's splendor.* The blessing was repeated directly below in Spanish.

"That's Eden *before* The Fall, of course."

"There was *no* fall, the way The Manor sees things. It's

a revisionist view." She offered her trademark sexy smirk. Her dark hair, cut short and straight and angled against her chin added to her devilish, pixie look. "Reality isn't welcome here," she said. "I told Carlos we should offer our wedding parties a two-for-one special. Their wedding reception in the grand ballroom, and one of our smaller rooms for their divorce celebrations, no matter how many years it takes."

"I'm glad you never lost your sense of hope."

"Couldn't live without it."

The bar area was done entirely in black: vinyl booths, floor tiles, walls dotted with silver star-like sequins, and the bar itself—long and sleek and polished to an obscenely high gloss. She ordered us coffee, asked how life had been treating me.

"Pretty much the same guy you knew back when."

"That's good. I *pretty much* liked who you were."

"We're supposed to evolve with time, aren't we?"

"Into what?"

"Something better."

She gave me an amused smile. "We are who we are."

"You don't think we can change?"

"I think the core remains. We put different dresses on it."

She sat there in her crisp tailored blouse, smiling, mischief again in her eyes. Once on one of our double-dates we were alone in my car, waiting for Vera. Sue had leaned back to stretch, her short skirt riding up on her legs which were parted and moving ever so slightly closer then away from each other. She took my hand and placed it on the soft flesh of her thigh. I left it there no more than a moment before withdrawing it; but that moment's hesitation seemed to be reflected in the smile she was offering now.

"I didn't mean to blindside you like that on the phone."

"You didn't," she said quickly, the composed and savvy business woman again. "As soon as I heard your voice I knew why you were calling, that you'd heard about Vera. I was shocked Norm had reached out to you. I wouldn't have expected it."

"You know him well?"

"Well enough. Though most of the time I got together with Vera it was only the three of us."

"The *three* of you?"

"Vera, Devon and I. We did a lot together."

Her face softened. If I didn't know her better, I would have likened it to a maternal glow.

"That kid was wonderful. I loved being around him almost as much as she did."

She waited while an intern brought us coffee.

"He had this kooky sense of humor, he could laugh at almost anything, and when he laughed you felt good in a way you never had before. There was no way you couldn't laugh with him."

Her eyes had glazed over. "He especially loved playgrounds. He'd stay on the swings till your arms were too sore to push him, giggling and going *whoo-whoo* as he went higher and higher. His arms spread out so his little hands could catch the wind. I think he saw himself as a train flying through the clouds. The *whoo-whoo* was the train whistle."

Her eyes now, moist at the corners. "And the see-saw. He thought it was the funniest thing when the plank hit the ground and his little butt would bounce hard. He loved the bump. *Bump-itty bump bump*, he called it. He kept wanting to do it over and over until his butt hurt too much and he told us to stop."

She was lost to memory, before pulling herself back, and speaking more matter-of-factly. "His favorite thing, though, was what he called his fly-walk. Vera would take one arm, and I the other. We'd lift him a few inches off the ground and walk down the street like that, Devon between us with his feet dangling in the air and a grin as wide as his face."

She looked to see how I was taking it. "I sound like he was my own child, don't I?"

"I haven't seen that side of you before. You see, we *can* change."

"Not really."

"What about Davison? I couldn't get a good read on his feelings for the boy. There was almost no trace of him in their house."

"I think Norm resented Devon precisely because Vera loved him so much, and of course because Devon was the way he was."

"So she was raising the boy on her own?"

"More or less." She thought a moment before adding, "I don't want to condemn the man. I mean, it wasn't easy for him. I don't think he knew what to do with a child like Devon. When she was pregnant he tried to talk her into having tests done. She wouldn't hear of it. She'd had two miscarriages already and the tests increase the likelihood of that, if only by ten percent or so. She told me she'd rather have a deformed child than no child at all."

"So why wouldn't she have kept mementoes, something more than a coffee mug with the boy's name on it?"

"Her will, or lack of it."

"Meaning—?"

"After Devon died, she stopped fighting Norm. If he wanted to erase the boy from their lives, she let it happen. That's my guess, anyway. She stopped caring what he did." She sipped from her cup and set it gently down on the saucer. "Did he tell you about her other disappearing acts?"

"No."

"She's done it before. A day here, a night there. Since Devon died."

"Did she ever say where she went, what she did?"

"She called them her secret journeys, her private time."

"What about recently? Did she give any hint she might be leaving again?"

She hesitated before saying, "I haven't seen her much lately. But no, the last time we met she was pretty much the way she's been since Devon died, a little depressed, a little distant."

"So there was nothing she said or did, nothing at all, that would indicate where she might be now?"

"I don't think so. I'm—I'm a pretty good listener." After a moment, she added, "I don't think she's been happy for a while now. Norm comes across as one of the nicer guys in this world. But there's so much he didn't know about Vera, didn't even think to ask. A woman's got to be *seen* to feel loved."

Again I wondered: *If she'd been unhappy, why wouldn't she—why hadn't she contacted me*?

I fingered the coffee cup, stared at the now cold black liquid. "Did Vera ever mention the Blue Flower?"

There was a silence before she said, "No. Not that I recall. Why are you asking?"

"She mentioned it in her journal."

Another hesitation. "She had her private side, that's for sure. She didn't tell me everything she did. Who knows? Maybe it was some yoga group, or some New Age spirituality thing. It could mean anything."

"The Blue Flower awaits. Do we dare a rendezvous with death?"

"What? What are you asking me?"

"That's what Vera wrote in her journal."

"We know she has the soul of a poet."

"Poems have meanings, don't they?"

Sue said nothing.

Silence, I was thinking, feels heavier in an all-black room.

"So you don't think she's in danger?"

She smiled at that, a quiet, knowing smile that implied more than she was saying. "There's always danger, isn't there? Either from the world—or ourselves."

20

Standing stiffly in his living room, Davison looked uncomfortable, not unlike the way he'd first appeared outside my door. He was wearing horn-rimmed glasses behind which his eyes seemed to falter with apology, at odds with the quiet elegance of his thin, patrician face.

I'd come in on the offensive. My annoyance at him overshadowing Vera's lingering presence in this cluttered room. "These vanishing acts," I asked. "How often do they occur?"

"Not often."

I studied his face for duplicity. Was the vagueness hiding something or was he simply an absent-minded professor, his focus more on hypotheses and theories than on the realities of everyday life? "What does that mean, *not often*?"

"It's happened a few times."

"How many?"

"Four times before this. This is the fifth."

"And you say this is the longest she's been away?"

"She's never been away for more than one night."

"Then what happens?"

"Nothing."

"*Nothing?*"

"She refuses to talk about it." He thought a moment. "She always seems calmer when she returns. Less troubled. For a few days, at least."

"I thought you said she'd been acting ordinary again after rehab, that she'd gotten back to normal."

"That *was* normal for Vera. Off and on moodiness. She's always been like that as long as I've known her."

"And then what happens?"

"It's life as usual. She goes back to taking photographs. We go on."

"Do you see any pattern? Something that might trigger it? These vanishing acts."

"Nothing I've figured out so far." A moment, then, "Other than they've all occurred *after* Devon died. Twice before rehab, the others after."

"I can't believe you wouldn't try to get her to explain."

"I did try."

"And?"

"She'd clam up. It only made it worse if I pushed. So I let it go," Davison confessed with the now familiar trace of apology in his eyes. "What else could I do?"

I could think of a hundred things a man could do. "Why didn't you tell me this? Why did I have to wait to hear it from Sue?"

"Because this time it's different," he said with a level gaze. "Because she hasn't come back." No apology now. "That's why I waited before coming to you. To be certain this wasn't like the other times."

"You still should have told me."

"You're right. I see that now. I should have known better."

"In her journal she mentioned something called the Blue Flower. Any idea what that is?"

"Some sort of horticultural thing, I assume."

"Was she into gardening?"

"She puttered around a bit. In the backyard."

I hesitated before asking, "Is it possible she left voluntarily?"

He turned on me with a hurt, disbelieving look. "Is that what Sue thinks?"

I chose my words carefully. "Without Devon, was she unhappy enough to—?"

"To leave me?"

"I'm trying to explore all possibilities." But even those words, gentle as I thought they were, did little to assuage the offense he'd taken.

"If that were true," he said, "I wouldn't want to go on living. Despite never having forgotten you, she loved it here. This house, this neighborhood, her photography. She was looking forward to getting back to teaching again in the fall."

His conviction grew stronger as he spoke.

"She knows she can count on me for support, while she works through her problems. She knows how reliable I am. I've stood by her all this time. She wouldn't have just vanished like that, unless she was kidnapped or abducted. I'm absolutely sure of it."

21

Night again.

Reading Vera's journal.

Her son, Devon, told her once he had a secret. But when she asked what it was, he couldn't remember. At first she wondered if he was withholding something from her, that his admission suggested a deeper level of intelligence, filling her with hope, but he never mentioned it again. Whenever she would ask, he would say, "No secrets, Mommy. No secrets. Just you and me."

After that particular story I came upon a single reference, perhaps to Davison though his name wasn't mentioned. If I was interpreting the symbolism correctly, it seemed to corroborate Sue Quinn's declaration that the man had wanted little to do with his child. *He lives in too narrow a world*, Vera wrote, *to admit the presence of light. Such a strange but beautiful light.*

I got up to pour a whiskey.

3 a.m.

Nite Hawk time.

Angie, a toll taker on the Tri-Boro Bridge, saying she'd been working the overnight shift for three years now and it had given her a lot of time to think. About money, for example. How much of it passed through her hands in the course of her shift and how unimportant it seemed at those hours of the night, "What with that cold wind blowin' offa the river, nothin' for company but the sound a tires on pavement and a couple words here and there when the driver-side window gets rolled down. Sometimes a smile. Sometimes a curse. Sometimes nothin' but a blank stare."

She'd come to believe what you saw in people in daylight was a mask. The true self was revealed only in the dead of night. "And ya know what gets me through them nights?" she asked.

"The sunrise. Geez, yeah. Like a promise I can count on. I wait for it the way you wait for a dream come true. The way the sky over Queens shatters up all pink and yellow and orange light, the way them colors reach across the water till the silver struts of the bridge burn with a light so blind you can't but hardly bear to look. Like being warmed by the heart of this sad, old universe. If it wasn't for that, geez, I don't know. I just don't know—"

I was reminded of the late-night waiter in a Hemingway story, the man musing on the emptiness of the universe: *It was all a nothing and man was nothing too. It was only that and light was all it needed. . . .*

I pushed aside the half-empty glass, left the radio on. Voices to return to.

On the street, walking uptown, I passed shuttered bars, darkened storefronts.

The Park Drive was closed to vehicular traffic. The silence of trees and grass. On benches hidden from the road, shadows shifting. Voices floating in the dark.

I wasn't what I'd call a fearful man, except in the way most life-long New Yorkers are fearful. Never leaving my car unlocked. Always keeping tabs on my surroundings. Trusting my sixth-sense to detect danger.

The fact of the matter was this: the self was the enemy I feared most, not strangers on the street.

Past Tavern On the Green where once, in that other lifetime, I'd taken Vera to lunch.

Past Belvidere Castle where like royalty in our self-conceived fairy tale, we spent stolen afternoons, surveying our kingdom below: the turtle pond, dark and motionless, a thick clot of weed-smothered water, and beyond that the rust-colored dirt of the baseball diamonds barely visible against the darker swath of outfield grass, and farther still the sputtering line of traffic glimpsed between the trees along Fifth Avenue. *There's magic here*, she liked to say. *Whatever we wish for in our wildest dreams.*

Past the lake and the Bow Bridge. It was the bridge I'd

recognized in several of Vera's photographs, the bridge where one night in an act of heedless daring, she had climbed onto its stone railing. Before that, at her insistence, we'd made love again in the tunnel. She liked the risk involved. Not that she wanted to be seen, but the possibility of it excited her. Afterward the bridge presented another dare. The railing was rounded, making it difficult to balance. Once there, the water of the lake some fifteen feet below, she became unsteady, the look on her face changing from bravado to fear.

I opened my arms, reached out to her.

It was the first time I'd said to her the words: *Just let go and come to me.*

I said them again to reassure her, *Just let go.* Then I said: *I'll be here when you fall.*

One more promise I never got to keep.

Now an occasional street lamp illuminated the path with a narrow blue light. Ahead was the tunnel of our love.

A hollow of darkness in the greater dark.

Memory and the present moment becoming one.

Whatever I hoped to find seemed right beyond reach. Some trace of Vera in the air, in the stone. Some fragment of memory that might explain why I'd lost her. Or why she had become this new woman I was getting to know—not quite a stranger, not quite an old friend. But that was wishful thinking, I told myself. What happened here between us happened in another lifetime. It had no bearing on the present.

Oh but it does, it does, an inner voice chided. *The past has everything to do with this present moment. The past is the present by another name*.

In the hard beating of my heart, I could sense—despite my resistance—the truth of that.

22

Fate falls heaviest on those in love.

How else to explain what happened when I came out of the park, walking south on Central Park West.

Birds beginning their reveille in the trees beyond the wall.

A figure emerging from the shadows of that wall, asking me what I needed, what I wanted.

"Nothing *you* can give me."

"This time a night man's got to need *somethin'*. Help him through. See it in your eyes, the way you're walkin'."

I waved him away but he persisted, dogging me half a block or more, keeping up a steady patter. "Know who I am? I'm the messenger, the angel of salvation. Got what you want. Sure do. Got any kind a help you need, man. Got the best there is. Got the Blue Flower."

I stopped abruptly, turned to him: a dim face darkened by the hoodie he was wearing. "What is it?"

"Best high there is, man. Best high you ever gonna get. Money back guarantee."

I gave him the twenty dollars he wanted for the small glassine bag. Under a street lamp, I held it to the light. Fine white powder. A long-stemmed pale-blue flower stenciled on the bag's upper right corner.

"Where—?" But when I turned he was gone, having slipped through an entrance to the park.

The walkway curved downward. Where the trees fell away toward the bottom of the hill I saw him crossing flat ground, moving in the direction of the reservoir. Briefly he was lost to the shadows, then he re-appeared passing through a cone of light on the bridle path.

He must have been moving even faster than I thought because I didn't catch sight of him again until he was close to the 97th Street transverse. His shadow figure crossed the road and that was the last I saw of him.

I'd been running, my breath coming in short, quick gasps and I stared uncertainly at the possibilities the various paths presented.

I passed a recreation complex with basketball courts, more ballfields. Then I was walking along the edge of a large meadow that brought me to Fifth.

A few cars moving uptown into Harlem, no pedestrians in sight.

Little hope of finding him now but still I walked north as far as 125th, before giving up and hailing a cab.

On the way downtown, tight in my hand, the glassine bag like a deviant grail.

23

Beneath Washington Square Park's stone arch, an *a capella* group sang about hearts on fire, hearts of stone. At the fountain children played in the wading pool beside signs forbidding that. No poets declaiming, but there were readers of poetry perched on the low wall surrounding the fountain.

Jack Connelly, a former NYPD precinct captain, sat on his usual bench facing the fountain. Years ago I'd met him at a writers' conference where he was lecturing on crime scene forensics; he was my source when I needed details about police matters. Keeping me honest, those times my imagination wanted to ignore reality for the sake of moving the plot forward.

Retired, he came to the park with his Yankees cap pulled low, eyes hidden behind wraparound shades. "Lots of memories here in the Village," he'd explained to me once, "that's why I still come down. But an ex-cop's not always welcome. No way you didn't leave some folks pissed as hell."

He suggested we walk, "stretch the old bones" was his way of putting it, "despite this damn knee of mine." Though only in his mid-fifties, he'd been using a cane of late.

An easy stroll around the fountain.

Everyone, it seemed, moving faster than we were: cyclists, skateboarders, students hunched beneath backpacks.

"You don't look good," he said.

"Late night."

"Hope she was worth it."

I let the irony of that go unacknowledged. "You know anything about the Blue Flower?"

"Yeah. Used to be what they called some no-name dive in the Alphabet. Cop hangout. Lots of Narcs. Never went there myself, but I knew guys who did."

"Is it still around?"

"No idea. Like I said I never went there."

"It's a brand of heroin being sold on the street now."

"Shows how out of it I am." He laughed at himself, pressing forward on his cane. "Kind of curious, though, don't you think?"

"You think there's a connection?"

"Far be it from me to impugn my fellow officers."

"But—?"

"Hey, I didn't say a thing."

"But—?"

He stopped to lean heavily on his cane. Though a man known for his reserve, a brief perverse flicker of his lips gave him away. "Things do happen, don't they?"

24

On a forlorn block between C and D, surrounded by abandoned buildings and vacant lots, what I found was an unpainted wooden relic of a building, two-story western-style porch and all. No name out front.

Connelly's directions had been vague but this had to be the place. No other operating business near it. For the length of the block, broken-down chain-link fences served as barriers between the trash on the street and the trash in the overgrown yards.

Under the awning of an abandoned tenement, windows hollowed out, front door hanging open and half off its hinges, I waited. No one came in or out of the bar. Until a black Caddy pulled up. A big man in grey sweats stepped out and went inside. Within minutes, he re-emerged, walking head down back to his car.

My angle was a side view; I couldn't see his face clearly. Still, there was something familiar. The walk, the way he carried his shoulders.

The Caddy throbbed into life, made a left on D, chrome glinting in the sun, and headed north.

Again I waited. Half an hour. Nothing.

Inside, the bar was empty. Dark as the street was bright. Smelling of dust and mold. Thin shafts of silver light from its two windows piercing the gloom.

The barkeep—broad-faced, silver hair combed back straight—watched me trip on the two steps leading down. "How we tell the regulars from the newbies. No need to look at the face. Just listen for a shoe slippin' and slidin'."

"Must keep you in lawsuits."

A half-laugh, half grunt response. "No law in the Alphabet. Least that used to be true. Before they decided the land had condos written all over it."

"This place have a name?"

"Not since I been working here."

"How long is that?"

"Awhile."

He brought a beer and retired to the end of the bar behind a copy of the *Daily News*, leaving me to take in the place and wonder what, if anything, it had to do with Vera.

The opposite wall, crammed as it was with photographs, each picture in a neat black frame, caught my attention. Beer in hand, I moved along it. The first of the photos showed signs of age, faded or fading black & white images, a few even sepia-toned. Closer to the restrooms at the back, the photos were in color, sharper in detail.

The photos, at least those that I first looked at, were mostly of men—lined up at what was clearly this bar, in groups of two or three or four, all smiles, arms around each other or their hands raised, each holding a drink. I recognized the man in the Caddy in more than a few. Always surrounded by men who seemed to be celebrating something. And now, seeing him full face and up close, I remembered him as Sue Quinn's date, those few times we'd gone out together. It took a moment before the name came to me. Mike something. Mike Monahan.

Beyond the men's room, among what appeared to be even more recent photos, was one of four men and a woman. All of them sat staring up at the camera from the bar's one and only table. The men were smiling, the woman was not.

Despite the poor light, there was no doubt the woman was Sue Quinn. Her eyes flat, expressionless. Her mouth, though, was drawn tight with annoyance.

The men wore dress shirts, open collar, no ties. Sue wore a black leather jacket, faux motorcycle style, and a pair of tight jeans. Certainly the photo went back a few years, but how many years was harder to pinpoint.

Some movement out of the corner of my eye. The barkeep, still holding the paper, was watching me.

I tipped my glass toward him, smiled. "Like your photo gallery. Goes back over the years, doesn't it?"

Again a half-grunt, half-mumbled response. "Place has been around a while, yeah."

He studied me for several seconds before going back to his paper and I turned my attention again to the photos. A series of them that were sharp and clean, *recent*.

In one, Sue appeared again with another woman. The man between them, with an arm around each of them, was Mike Monahan. His smile was broad, triumphant. The smiles of the two women less so.

The other woman in the photo was Vera.

The barkeep's face was buried in the newspaper. As a shield, I pulled open the door to the men's room before removing the photo and the tack that held it, as well as the one with Sue and the group of men.

Inside the men's room, I studied the one with Vera. It appeared to have been taken around the same time as the photo in Davison's living room. Her hair was the same length. Her smile had a similar forced quality. In this one, though, she was all made up. Lipstick, eye-shadow, dangling ear rings. Things that, when I knew her, she paid scant attention to. That, and the black cocktail dress she wore, suggested it was a night out on the town.

I lingered a few seconds more leaning against the door before reaching over to flush one of the urinals.

At the bar, I ordered another beer and drank it slowly. Not the kind of place you asked questions about the clientele. Not if you wanted answers. But I held up the photo of Vera that Davison had given me. "Have you seen this woman recently?" I asked. "Her picture's on the wall down there."

The barkeep glared at me over the newspaper. He didn't bother to look at the photo in my hand. "I wouldn't know," he said.

"She's a friend of mine. I'm trying to reach her."

His face was hidden again behind the newspaper. "Like I said, I wouldn't know."

Behind him, above the bar itself and sitting on the upper-most shelf, reflected in the dull and clouded ancient mirror, was a vase with an over-sized plastic blue flower, its petals spread wide.

25

"It's a cruise to the moon," Connelly said over the phone. "That Blue Flower shit. Hell of a high, from what I'm told, over-the-top potent. A big deal on the lower East Side, which is where—apparently—a lot of it's being sold."

"You know a cop, ex-cop maybe, name of Mike Monahan?"

"Yeah, I knew him. He retired last year, what I hear. Why, he in the high-end pharmaceutical trade now?"

"Might he be?"

"Might's a wide-open word. A world of possibility in those five letters."

"That's what I'm asking."

"No idea what the guy's into now. But could he be dirty? Sure. There were rumors."

"Meaning—?"

"Internal Affairs brought him in once or twice. Never got charged, though."

He sucked in his breath, let the air out slowly. "I kinda got dragged into working with the guy on a few occasions, when they were short-handed. Up in the Bronx, before I made Captain. They pulled me off firearms a couple nights here and there to work undercover. A ghost, see. Means you're on the street in plain clothes as back-up when something's going down—a bust, a shakedown, whatever. Which is real risky because most of the time you're *not* undercover, you're visible to the community. So on one of these night raids, when you're workin' backup, if you get recognized by someone on the street you're dead meat. And with Monahan's raids there was always something weird going on."

He drew in his breath again, a half-sigh. "Worst night was I was a ghost at Baychester up in the Bronx, hanging out by the playground. They were goin' in after this drug lord, leader of a local gang who was supposed to be at his girlfriend's apartment on the second floor of Building 1621. My job's to be on the lookout for the rest of the crew, 'cause if they show up we're in deep shit. Major fireworks. Bullets flyin' every which way.

"So I'm just some guy out for a smoke, leaning against a lamp post. The entire move's supposed to be bang bang, they go in, break down the door, grab the guy. But that's not the way it went down. I mean they got the guy, they're sneakin' him out the basement door but Monahan's still in there for God knows what reason. I can't leave my post till he comes out and gives the all clear. Meantime the entire crew shows up, they got word somehow, and sure as hell one of them makes me, starts running toward me shouting, then all of them, fifteen, twenty guys are comin' at me. I'm running my ass off, down the middle of the street, I mean these guys'll crucify me. I never been so scared in my life and I been in some bad situations, let me tell you. I'm sayin' my prayers 'cause I know I'm not going to make it to the avenue. No way, too far. I'm already outta breath, these guys are gainin' on me, I mean these are young guys, teenagers, twenty-somethings, no way am I gonna outrun them, and then a squad car comes screeching in from the avenue, saves my ass."

His voice had taken on a slight wheeze. "Monahan. What the hell was he doing staying back like that? I coulda been torn apart limb by limb. For what? Some bullshit deal he was working with whoever was left in the apartment?" His voice came louder now, thick with exasperation. "That's the way he was. Ballsy as hell. Always something unexpected like that. What the hell was he doing in there? I still don't know. But I'd lay odds whatever it was, it wasn't legit."

He caught his breath before adding, "So yeah, to answer your question is he dirty. It's not beyond the realm of possibility."

26

Sue didn't answer her phone, but called me back an hour later. I told her I'd found out what the Blue Flower was.

Silence. A drawn breath.

When I explained, she said in a flat voice, "Oh."

"Do you think Vera was using?"

"Not as far as I know."

"But you said you hadn't had much contact with her lately. Could she have started without you knowing?"

"Is this a cross-examination?"

"Sorry," I said. "I'm not accusing you of anything."

"Sounds like you are."

"I'm trying to get at the truth."

"I'm aware of that."

I waited before asking, "Did she go to bars?"

"Vera? You kidding?"

"I'm asking."

"Not that I know of. Unless she picked up the habit lately. When Devon was alive, she was always at home. And after, she wasn't in much of a party mood." After a moment, she asked, "What makes you think she did?"

"Nothing. Trying to make sense of things, that's all."

I lifted the bar photo of Sue, Vera and Monahan from my desk and held it to the light. Clearly the photo was a recent one, clearly the bar with its clouded mirror was the one I'd visited that afternoon. "That guy you were dating, that cop, Monahan—"

"That was over. Years ago."

"Any idea what he might be doing now?"

"Why would I?"

"Just curious, that's all."

"He's a mean son-of-bitch. You don't want to get mixed up with him."

"*You* did."

"Yeah, well, we all make mistakes," she said coldly.

Again I gave her time to make an admission, volunteer something. Again, her silence.

"We should get together," I said. "Talk some of this over. I'm a bit stuck at the moment."

"As I've said, maybe she doesn't want to be found."

"I can't leave it that way. Not without knowing for sure."

"You can't let things go, can you?"

"Meaning what?"

"Meaning sometimes the smartest thing is to forget the past."

27

I was staring down at the courtyard trying to figure Sue's angle when Davison called to say he'd checked again with the police.

Still nothing.

I drew a breath and exhaled softly, easing into what had been troubling me. "Was it only alcohol Vera abused? Could she have been into drugs, as well?"

Davison's voice tightened. He said as if it were an accusation, "What kind of drugs?"

"Heroin possibly."

"Not a chance! I would have known if she was."

Would you? I was thinking. "It's only a question," I said in a conciliatory tone. "A hypothesis."

"Why would you even *think* that?" Davison couldn't control the hostility in his voice.

"A hypothesis, like I said. There's a reference in Vera's journal to the Blue Flower. It's a form of heroin being sold in the city these days. I'm exploring every possibility."

"Well, you're wrong on this one. Totally off-base."

"I hope I am. I don't want to think that of her any more than you do." Truth was, I was sick as hell over it. I tried a different tack. "Did Vera ever say anything about Sue Quinn being into drugs?"

"Why, is she a junkie too?"

Again, I backed away from the man's hostility. "I'm looking at everything, that's all."

"You want me to ask Sue directly?"

"No. No. That wouldn't be a good idea. I'll ask when the time comes." Some cards you want to hold. This was one of them. "Besides," I added, "Sue said she hadn't spent much time with Vera lately. She might not have known if Vera had developed a habit."

"I don't know why she would have said that. The week or two before Vera disappeared they were on the phone, it seemed, every other day." He hesitated, then added, "I'm exaggerating, but it seemed like they were back and forth a lot. And those calls at odd hours. I suspected Sue might be one of the callers."

Another of Sue's deceptions. Or, at best, half-truths.

Several moments of silence passed before Davison with a less bellicose edge asked, "What else have you found?"

"Nothing definite."

"Nothing to help put my mind at ease?"

"Afraid not."

"Let's meet," he suggested. "Put our heads together. I'm going crazy here worrying."

28

The cemetery where Devon was buried spread out alongside the Cross Bronx Expressway, the ceaseless rushing sound of moving traffic blowing like wind across the broad, flat acres of gravestones.

I'd been there before, years back, with Vera. She wanted to visit the grave of her favorite singer, Billie Holiday, who was buried in a section at the far end of the cemetery near 177th Street.

"You probably think I'm morbid," Vera said, holding a bouquet of gardenias, the signature flower Holiday wore in her hair when she performed. "I mean, wanting to come here like this."

"*Curious*," I said, "*devoted*. Not morbid."

"Norm would say it's foolish, serving no purpose."

Whatever thoughts I had about her husband, I kept to myself. If I'd been a more honorable man, if I'd possessed a stronger will, I would have stayed away from getting involved with her. The least I could do, I told myself, was to not take sides. So I sidetracked the issue, saying simply, "One of the things I like about you. Your curiosity. Always a new world to explore. Besides, my parents made graveyard visits at least once a month. Usually, though," I added with a laugh, "to relatives, family friends, people they knew."

"But I *do* know her. I've read all about her life. I have all of her records. I know the lyrics to every song she sang, the most famous ones anyway." Her face flushed. Self-conscious, a hint of embarrassment. A look that accompanied her more personal revelations.

We stood before the modest granite monolith, the name HOLIDAY at the top, centered above an embedded cross. Beneath the cross an open Bible with the words, *Hail Mary, Full of Grace* etched into the stone.

In a soft reverent voice, she read the inscription to the left of the cross. “Beloved daughter, Billie Holiday.” The singer was buried with her mother, Sadie, whose brief inscription—first name only and her dates—was written on the right side of the cross.

It seemed too ordinary a resting place for such a luminous performer.

I wondered, as all writers must, if anything I wrote would ever inspire a reader to visit *my* grave, wherever that might turn out to be. “Why her?” I asked. “I mean, of all the singers in the world.”

“She was an only child, like me,” Vera said. “I thought of her as a sister. Though my life was nowhere near as hard, or tragic.”

She recited some of Holiday’s troubles, a few of which I knew: that she was beyond poor, that as a child she ran errands for the women in a brothel who, in return, let her listen to their Louie Armstrong and Bessie Smith records—the way she learned how to sing. That as a teenager she sang twelve-hour shifts in Harlem clubs for two dollars a night, that she was addicted to alcohol *and* heroin, that she served time in prison, that the FBI and the police harassed her even while she lay sick and dying in her hospital bed. This last primarily because she’d sung a protest song about the lynching of young black men in the South. Vera stressed the point that Holiday, against all reason, was considered a threat to national security.

Her sigh came heavy with regret, indignation. “On top of everything else, she had such bad relationships with men. Whenever I was heartbroken, feeling sorry for myself, I’d listen to her sing *Lover Man* or *Good Morning, Heartache* or *Don’t Explain*. The range of emotion she could travel with her voice. She knew every tremor of love’s highs and lows.”

Kneeling on the grass, she lay the gardenias on the dry,

untended dirt in front of the stone. "Amazing, isn't it, that so much life and so much beauty, came out of so much pain."

"Not the prettiest place we could have chosen," Davison was saying as we walked toward Devon's grave at the newer end of the cemetery, "but it was one of the closest. Vera wanted him nearby. I would have preferred cremation, but she wouldn't hear of it. She saw it as too savage an act for a child—as she put it, for such a *gentle* child."

We walked on the grass bordering a long row of gravestones. The heart of the cemetery was treeless, graves naked under the sun, the rows nearly indistinguishable.

"I hadn't thought of it myself," Davison said, "but you're right. This is one of the places Vera would likely show up. *If* she's free and able to move about."

"That's one of the things we're trying to determine, isn't it?"

Davison strode briskly ahead of me, adamant still that she'd been taken away against her will.

Ahead of us, sunlight slivering off the crowns of tombstones. Solitary figures moving among the graves.

Davison raised his hand to shield himself from the glare. "Over here," he said.

Devon's grave. A small arched stone dwarfed by the larger stones on either side. A vase of yellow roses had been propped against the base of the stone. Davison gasped at the sight of it.

I knelt to examine the flowers, the petals drying out at the edges. A few days old, at least. The vase itself, translucent plastic, the kind any florist might dispense.

"Was there anyone else who might have put these here?"

"I can't imagine who," Davison said. "Yellow roses were what she brought each time we came."

"We know she's free to move around then, at least."

"Unless she was abducted *after* she came here. Perhaps this was her last act before—before it happened."

"You said the last time you saw her was at night, early evening about six o'clock, when she left for the park."

"That's right."

"Might she have come here instead? Might she have come here *after* the park? It would have been dark by then."

Davison shook his head in exasperation. "Knowing Vera, anything's possible. Maybe she was accosted right here. Teen age hoods, some homeless lowlife, whatever."

I stepped back then and it was Davison's turn to kneel. Bowing his head, one hand reaching to touch the stone. When he stood, he still kept one hand on the stone. The other held one of the roses. "When I come here, I just talk to him like I always did, parent-child kind of things, how to take care of himself, you know, like I was telling him to be careful crossing the street or to hold onto the banister when going down stairs."

I couldn't find the right words of comfort.

Davison stared down the long empty row of stones. "I should have done more for him. I don't know what, but I should have done more. For Vera, too." He looked at me in apology. "Graveyards bring out the regrets in us, I guess. Maybe that's their true purpose."

As we walked away, Davison said above the hiss of highway traffic, "It was going to be a hard life for him. I often thought he'd be better off dead." His face blanched at the admission. "God, I felt guilty as hell feeling that way, especially after he died; but that didn't change anything. I would never have admitted those feelings to Vera, not in a million years. She never would have forgiven me."

He looked at me with the same beseeching eyes as he had the night he first showed up in the courtyard. "We can't help feeling what we feel, can we?"

Observing parents and their children had always been something I did from a distance. Who was I to pass judgment?

He said with his familiar self-effacing shrug, "We are who we are."

"Seems so."

I couldn't help but like the man's honesty.

29

Davison said, “Do you mind if we stop in here?”

Outside the cemetery wall, alongside a row of elms, stood a stone chapel. Small, ancient, the inside smelling of must and dust and a lingering trace of incense. “When Vera got out of rehab,” Davison said, “she came here a lot. With me or alone. Each time she visited the grave. She told me the quiet helped her sort through the chaos.”

I stood at the back wall while he sat—still clutching the yellow rose, his body bent forward—on one of the flat wooden benches that served as pews.

Afternoon light threading spools of tinted mist through stained glass.

Shadows spreading silence.

The altar candles’ wavering glow.

A kind of peace, yes, but the Vera I knew would have laughed at this. “I said goodbye to the notion of the church as sanctuary when I graduated college,” she told me. One afternoon we’d driven upstate, made love on a rock ledge overlooking the Hudson Valley, trees and hills running on it seemed forever, eternal sky above.

She lay naked in my arms. Warm sun burning our skin. A thin breeze out of nowhere making her suddenly shiver against me. “Who needs a church when we have this? Heaven is ours right here.” In a mocking voice, she added, “Imagine being made in the image and likeness of God.” That tickled her no end. “Our pathetic, scrawny little bodies and minds with their multitudes of imperfections created in God’s image. What kind of God would that be?”

“It’s hard to believe she returned to the church,” I said when Davison rose from the wooden bench.

“I’m not certain that *returned* is the right word. It’s more like she found some kind of peace here, something she couldn't get anywhere else. I think it was a way of feeling closer to Devon." He shrugged then in another gesture of self-effacement. "But who am I to say? I don't understand these things."

"Faith, you mean?"

"In my world, everything has to be proven."

Spinning light from the windows, like a form of grace, fell upon the flat wooden seats. If I were a believer, I might think the light was a sacred intrusion, mocking hollow men like myself and the darkness we lived in. "Is there a priest here she was close to? Someone we can talk to?"

Davison shook his head. "From what she told me she kept to herself when she came here. It wasn't the living she was trying to reach."

Outside I asked him if the name Mike Monahan meant anything to him.

His head jerked up in surprise. "The cop?"

"Yes."

"Friend of Sue Quinn's, yes. Funny you should bring him up. He called Vera, after Devon died. And we ran into him a few times *accidentally*, or so he claimed. Made me feel awkward as hell."

"Why's that?"

Davison shrugged. "His attitude, I guess. It was like I wasn't there. He'd talk to Vera like they were old friends. Like they had some exclusive history together." He thought about it some more. "He seemed like the bullying sort, hard as nails. Someone you might hire as a bodyguard. Someone to fight your battles."

"Did Vera say anything about him?"

"Only that she didn't like him. She couldn't understand why Sue ever went out with him. Why do you ask?"

"He seems to have a connection to both Sue *and* Vera."

"In what way?"

"I don't yet know that." I deliberated telling him about the photo from the bar. Instead I said, "He was interested in them both."

"Romantically, you mean?"

"That's part of it, at least."

"It certainly wasn't reciprocal. Not on Vera's part, in any case."

So it would seem, I thought.

Davison stared down at the yellow flower in his hand. "It's foolish, I know, but I think I'll keep this. It's the most recent thing I have of hers."

He tucked it delicately into the pocket of his jacket.

30

Turned out, Mike Monahan still lived in the Bronx, not far from the cemetery. A drab pre-war tenement on a street of tenements. When he swung open the door, he stared at me dull-eyed. A moment passed, before memory took hold. "How the hell'd you find me?"

The phone book had no listing for him.

No idea, Sue had said when I asked about his whereabouts. So I'd taken a chance—we'd picked him up here on one of our double-dates. "From the old days."

He grunted in a dismissive way, as if to say he'd long ago erased that part of his life.

"It's about Vera," I said. "She's disappeared."

Neutral expression, hint of a scowl. No telling if he was surprised.

With a non-committal wave of his arm, he turned away, moving ahead of me down a narrow hall that widened into a living room, the place only slightly brighter and less dingy than the floor landing. Light came from a single casement window, the edges of the room in shadow. In those shadows a bedroom door stood open, revealing an unmade bed, clothes strewn here and there on the floor. The smell of something sour, overcooked—cabbage maybe—drifted from the kitchen.

If he was dirty, he sure as hell wasn't spending his illicit gains on his digs.

Heavier, grayer, he let himself sink into an armchair by the window, as if even that small amount of effort, walking to and from the front door, had annoyed him. Glass of whiskey in hand, he made no attempt to conceal he was sizing me up. "You haven't changed much."

It wasn't a compliment.

Mid-afternoon like this, in his rumpled sweater and what

looked to be a pair of worn-out gray uniform pants, he sprawled rather than sat in the chair—anchored there, it would seem from his deepening scowl, by bitterness. A man from whom life was still holding something back. A contrast to the man sporting those triumphant smiles on the walls of the Blue Flower bar.

"What's her disappearance got to do with you?" he said.

I'd been taking in the room. Book shelves with no books, only photos. Monahan in his younger days, uniformed and slimmer, at various police functions. One of him in a black tux at a banquet looking as though he'd won the lottery, and one of him older, dressed in a sport jacket, accepting an award. Nothing, it seemed, taken at the Blue Flower; but in each photo, an arrogance characterized his look. In his eyes, defiance burned like an eternal flame.

The same guy I remembered.

Photos of Vera were tucked in among the others: Vera walking on the street. Going into or coming out of stores. Entering the chapel Davison had taken me to. Having coffee at an outdoor café. Standing by the boat pond in Central Park, looking down at the water from Bow Bridge, her camera strapped across her shoulder.

Surveillance photos. Taken from some distance.

Back then, our double-dating days, it was no secret: he had a thing for her. We all knew that. But this, unholy though it was, seemed like a shrine.

He said again, "What's it got to do with you?" An edge in his voice, daring me to say something about the photos.

I stood there uncertainly, not having been invited to sit. "Wondering when was the last time you saw her."

"What's that to you?"

"Her husband's asked me to find her."

No effort to hide his disdain. "Why would he do that?"

"He thinks I can be of help. He thinks she's in some kind of danger."

Something registered in the former detective's eyes. He shifted in his seat. I waited, hoping he might volunteer something, but he simply glared back at me.

"That's why I was wondering if you'd seen her, if she'd given any hint where she might be."

"You think I'd tell you if I had?"

"I don't know. Would you?"

"Why the hell would I?"

"We both cared about her." I couldn't think of a better argument. "We both want to know she's all right, don't we?"

Monahan sneered at that.

"Not sure why you're still so angry."

"You're a piss-ant, that's why." The man took a long swallow of whiskey, then held the glass in front of him, staring into it before he raised his eyes. "I don't waste my time with losers. Like Davison. Or you." He reached for a cigarette and lit it with a Zippo, drew deep, not taking his eyes from me. "You think you're up to the task? Finding her?"

"We'll see, won't we?"

Monahan regarded me warily. "You want my honest, you're no detective. No matter what bullshit you write about. You never could figure out how the world works. You were always a two-bit dreamer."

"And what were you?"

"I deal with the world as it is."

And look at where it's gotten you, I held myself back from saying, *an overweight, past-his-prime ex- cop with a dirty rep*.

"Norm Davison said you'd called her." I decided not to mention the photo I'd taken from the wall of the Blue Flower. "I was hoping she might have said something, given some indication what was going on with her."

He waved his hand in dismissal, raising his glass and drinking as if I'd already left.

I stood in front of him, waiting for something more.

Finally he said, "You still here?"

So I gave up, started for the hall.

Monahan got to his feet, glass in hand, following me with a lurching step.

The door slammed behind me, cutting off the man's parting assault, "She thought you were a loser. She'd forgotten all about you years—"

From behind the door came a hacking sound, a cough that arose from deep in the chest. Except that it wasn't a cough at all, or maybe it had only begun as one.

The man was sobbing.

I wondered was it because he'd never gotten the woman he loved, or because he'd finally gotten her. And destroyed her.

31

Nightfall. The cemetery.

It seemed likely, if Vera had freedom of movement and didn't want to be found, she would make her visits under cover of darkness.

Enough room between the gate and the perimeter wall to squeeze through. Past a column of trees, the first rows of graves.

I watched for the flicker of shadows—the homeless seeking shelter for the night, teens getting high, those gangs and lowlifes Davison had alluded to—but except for an occasional skulking raccoon, at one point a family of five parading brazenly on the grassy carpet between graves, nothing moved save the occasional wind-rustle of leaves. At Devon's grave, the vase of yellow roses lay propped as we'd left it against the stone.

In the shadow of a lone oak, I waited. A long view: across the field of the dead to the far-off lights of the Whitestone Bridge. In between, the Bronx skyline thrust into smoky haze.

Waiting games like this made it easy for the mind to drift.

I was thinking about Eric, a Nite Hawk caller from some months back, who worked as a security guard at Greenwood Cemetery in Brooklyn. He'd never believed in ghosts, he said, until he began working the night shift there, making his rounds among the tombstones. I remembered his exact words. *Every shadow and every whisper of leaves or wind was a living thing. Resurrections were occurring all around me.*

Night, the ultimate trickster.

Maybe if I stayed long enough the same fate would befall me.

Somewhere I'd read about a remote tribe with unusual graveyard customs. The men in that society spent an entire night, from dusk till dawn, alone in the burial grounds. A rite of passage. They did this three times in the course of their life:

once at puberty, once in middle life, and once at age sixty. This was considered a purification; they had to confront themselves, their sins and their failings, before they could successfully move to the next phase of their life. What better place to do this than surrounded by the spirits of their ancestors and fellow-tribesmen. What better time than the black of night.

Above me, oak leaves lifting in the breeze.

Far-off, the mournful sound of expressway traffic.

Minutes slipping by, forever gone.

I began to see the point of the ritual. How it might be in this burial place, as hour moved against hour into the silence at the heart of the night. Framed against the seemingly endless aisles of the dead, all artifice was stripped away. A degree of nakedness not possible elsewhere.

Every shadow and every whisper of leaves or wind was a living thing.

In time—moments or hours, I couldn't tell which—it felt as if I was dissolving, neither man nor child but something significantly smaller, intangible and undefined. A hollow waiting to be filled.

Around me, tombstones emitting a grey luminescence.

Leaves whispering an incantation.

Shadows shape-shifting.

Lights of distant buildings inseparable from the stars.

The unceasing hum of traffic.

The restless song of dead souls.

So it seemed. So it seemed.

What I felt was an inescapable sense of remorse for the life I'd lived. Its solitude and lack of purpose.

Its barren core.

32

"You always call your friends in the dead of night?" Sue asked, her voice coquettish.

"It's not *that* late."

"Everything's relative." She exhaled softly, the luxuriant sound of someone stretched out in bed and comfortable.

"I'm not interrupting anything, am I?"

"Like what?" her voice flat, deadpan.

The Sue I remembered. Hard to know: Was she serious or playing with you? "Didn't figure you were the turn-in early type."

"It's past midnight, you know."

"Like you said, everything's relative."

"Besides," she went on, "you never took the opportunity to find out. Whether I turned in early or late, or not at all."

The kind of thing a woman says that there's no good answer to—unless, of course, you're interested in pursuing her.

From the phone booth where I stood outside the cemetery, I stared at the darkened flower shop across the street. The florist remembered the lady with the yellow roses. She come often, he'd said. The last time? He wasn't sure. One week, he thought. Maybe more, maybe less.

"Been wondering about things," I said.

"You're good at that. Wondering. I used to call you the Wonderer. One of my secret names for you."

"I won't ask you what the others were."

"And I wouldn't tell you, if you did."

Flirtation was never my specialty and, under the circumstances, I had no interest in playing games. I said nothing about Monahan or the Blue Flower, letting the silence hang between us, again hoping she would volunteer something.

Finally, I asked her if she knew anything about Vera's

church-going habits.

"Vigils," Sue said. "That's what she called them."

"Did she say anything about them? These vigils."

"Not really. I think they were more like private meditations, you know. Spending time alone with her grief. There was a priest she liked. At some church near the cemetery."

It stood not a hundred feet from the phone booth. Dark stone. Gothic spire that night turned into a foreboding presence.

"Does this priest have a name?"

"I don't think she ever mentioned it. Not that I can remember, at least. Just that he was someone she could talk to."

"You know more about her private life than Davison does."

Sue Quinn sighed. "Like I said, he's a well-meaning man."

"Blind, deaf and dumb too?"

"Now, now. Your jealousy's showing."

"I'm not jealous."

"No?"

I laughed. "Wouldn't admit it, if I was."

"Some things never change."

"Let's get together. Talk face to face." I was thinking, *It won't be as easy to lie to me that way.*

"I can't, Jake. There's a lot going on."

"What about now? A nightcap."

"No, tonight's not good."

"Tomorrow then."

"I've got a hell of a day tomorrow. Really."

"When then?"

"I'll let you know. Okay?"

Another deception, I was sure, amid a growing collection.

What she said next, despite her previous flirtations, took me off-guard.

"If you don't find her, or even if you do and it doesn't turn out to be what you're hoping for, come look for me."

Her voice had been flat and direct rather than playful. I

could picture her eyes, dark and intent and unswerving.

"I'll keep that in mind," I said before hanging up.

33

Davison's house was dark except for a light upstairs in the master bedroom.

The wooden porch. The gambrel roof. The cut stone of the early Dutch settlers. The white pine with heavy branches stretched above the guest room. I knew the place as if it were mine.

From the shadowed wall of a neighboring house, I couldn't take my eyes away.

I'd walked from the cemetery, a long walk, hoping to tire myself, to put to rest—for a few hours, at least—the envy that drove me.

A pilgrimage to a lost goddess.

I imagined Vera there, going about the details of ordinary life: cooking dinner, washing dishes, sitting on the sofa next to Davison, bringing him tea or coffee or a beer, turning down the covers before bedtime. Teaching Devon to stand, to walk, to say *I love you, Mommy.*

Nothing in its rightful place. Vera belonging to another man. A violation of some fundamental law, of what should have been the established order of the universe.

My universe. Vera at its center.

In matters of the heart we're all anarchists, aren't we?

The longer I stood there, the more fevered my thoughts. I felt even more of an interloper than when I first stepped inside their house. Then, at least, I'd been invited. What was my justification now? An intruder in the dark, on a street where I didn't belong, trespassing on the lives of others.

How did it all go wrong: this house, this street ripped from someone else's dream, Vera's life with Davison, both of them twisted figures in that dream I couldn't control. Something had been taken from me against my will and I'd come here this night to reclaim it.

What would I do? Smash the windows? Break down the door? Take Davison by the throat and demand what was rightfully mine be returned, insist those years be given back to me?

And then it was love that was driving me.

Vera and I together.

How many times? How many places?

Over the years when her presence was too strong to resist I'd recall each of them, re-live them moment by moment. That first time in the tunnel, the bed in my apartment, the countless times in the open air. By a lake, a river, a waterfall, our rocky ledge above the Hudson Valley. Each touch, each tremor. The nape of her neck when I pushed away her hair to kiss it, my finger tracing the smooth contours of her face—forehead, nose, lips, chin. The arch of her shoulders, the curve of her back. Her hips, her legs moving against me.

Was it the cool air of autumn that drove us indoors? Back to my apartment, then to this house.

Norm is away, she said. *We can stay here.*

We both knew it wasn't safe.

I want to, she said. *I want to.*

The guest room. The creaking branches outside the window, the brush of boughs against the windowpane. All night the smell of pine.

Time after time.

Afternoons, too. And mornings.

Whenever fate blessed us.

We didn't hear the key in the lock, the step on the stair. His figure in the doorway, watching.

Almost immediately, without a word, he turned away, descended the stairs.

Vera pulled on her jeans, her jersey top, ran after him barefooted.

From the window, through the branches of the pine, I saw him standing in the yard.

Shoulders rigid. His back to the house.

Vera running to him. Already leaving me. What should I have done to stop her? What *could* I have done?

Fool, I accused myself now, standing in the shadow of his neighbor's house.

No one took a thing from you.

You gave it away.

You loosened your hands and it vanished.

34

I needed someone to talk to.

Connie was turned toward the window with a vacant, far-off stare. On the table before her sat a nearly empty cup of coffee, a half-eaten slice of Key Lime pie. Past two in the morning at the Waverly diner on Sixth.

Sliding into the booth I said, "I was counting on your being here."

"That's me. Old Reliable." Her smile had more than its usual tinge of wry lament. She was still in costume: her blonde wig with its stiff, hair-sprayed curl over one eye, her tight form-fitting white T-shirt and red, pleated mini-skirt. In the bright unflattering light of the diner she looked like an aging kewpie doll.

She was one-third of the Belle Tones, a pop revival trio I'd been a fan of for several years now. On stage they used the names, Trixie, Dixie and Pixie and though they were in their late thirties they exuded a youthful and passionate energy. With their sexy, come-hither performance style they managed to evoke the legendary girl group era of the 50s and 60s—an era I'd come to know via my parents' record collection and the hours spent browsing through vintage record stores.

Dixie and Pixie had already turned in for the night so it was Connie alone who occupied this rear booth, the usual spot after their thrice weekly gig at the Neon Angel on Bleecker.

"What does Jakie need tonight?"

I'd known her almost eighteen months now and in that time not much had changed between us. When my writing was going badly I'd quit early and catch her last set at the Angel. On my loneliest nights I'd hang around afterward, buy her a drink, take her back to my place. For a while that arrangement seemed to have worked. Lately, though, she'd been hinting at something else.

"It isn't only about me, is it?"

"Mostly," she said. "Mostly it is."

Alphonse, the octogenarian waiter, stood beside the booth. "What can I bring you, Mr. Jake?"

"An espresso is fine."

"Double?"

"A single shot will do tonight. And another de-caf for Connie." I turned back to her, waiting, knowing more was coming.

She watched me, gauging how far she should go. "You come by on the nights *you're* feeling low. I don't know, it's like I don't exist for you the rest of the week."

"That's not true," I said lamely in my own defense.

"Isn't it?"

"No, I—"

"It feels like it is. It sure feels like it."

"I've been busy. Something's come up. I—I think about you, I do."

"Sometimes." She studied me as if she might be seeing me for the first time. "We always end up talking about *your* problems. Your books aren't selling the way you want them to, or your publisher is giving you a hard time, or you're feeling bored and abandoned because you've run out of ideas."

"Not always. It's not always my problems, is it?"

She lowered her eyes, said nothing while Alphonse brought coffee.

"Is it?" I pressed, once he'd left.

"No," she said softly.

"We talk about your problems, too."

"Once in a while," she acknowledged. "Once in a while we do." She seemed to be struggling to find some kind of balance. "You listen to me talk about how I'm in a rut, you do. You can be a good listener when you want to be. I tell you how my life doesn't change, doesn't seem to be getting anywhere, isn't building to something, a resolution or whatever, and how I'm afraid I'm going to grow old alone. And you tell me I should get out more, join a dating service, meet more men. But you don't really want me to meet men. Because if I met someone, I wouldn't be here when you need me in the middle of the night. Like this. So it really comes back to you again, doesn't it?

She watched me while I thought it over.

"I want what's best for you."

"You say that, but you don't really mean it. You want what's best for *you*. And what's best for you, or what you think is best for you, is for us to go on the way we do, using each other as a kind of Advil, temporary relief from our private hells." She watched me reach for the espresso, sip it slowly. "Don't you ever think we could possibly have more?"

"I told you—"

"I know, I know. You're a broken man. Something happened a long time ago that you never got over." She shook her head in regret. "All the men I go out with are broken. So I guess it's my fault. I'm the one picking them, right?"

"I'm sorry."

"For what?"

"For not giving you what you need."

"I don't even know what I need, so how could you?" Her eyes had lost their defensiveness. "You give me *something*, at least. Maybe you give me as much as I'm capable of receiving." She thought a moment. "Maybe I'm broken the same way you are, limited in terms of what I can take from the opposite sex." For a while she toyed with her coffee cup, turning it slowly in the saucer. "And that would be funny, wouldn't it? Me accusing you of what I'm just as guilty of. You'd have every right to be annoyed."

"I'm not annoyed."

"I know, I know. Mr. Equilibrium. Nothing gets to you, does it?"

"All I wanted was to talk a while."

A homeless man passed by outside the window, rapped hard on the glass, and grinned malevolently.

"Why tonight? Why is this all coming up tonight?"

"Why not tonight? It's as good as any night, isn't it?"

For that I had no answer. I drained the remaining coffee in my cup, set it carefully on its saucer. It seemed I'd been running into walls for days now. Connie, too. Apparently, the days had taken their toll on her, as well. Her face bore the weight of it. No pretense there. No stiff upper lip to mask the weariness.

I reached across the table to rest my hand on hers. She didn't pull away, but she didn't turn her hand palm up, as she normally did. It was simply my hand covering hers.

"You can call *me*, you know. You don't have to wait for me to call."

She shook her head no. "I'd feel I was interfering. With your writing."

"You wouldn't be interfering."

"With your private and apparently perpetual grief then."

"If you need me, call. Really."

The look in her eyes said she'd like to believe me, she really would, but she'd been through too much in her life to buy it.

I rubbed my thumb gently over the back of her hand, watching her watching me.

No other customers at the moment. Too late for mid-week party-goers, too early for the pre-dawn breakfast crowd. Near the door, Alphonse sat at a table, head tipped forward, dozing.

The silence of the hour descended upon us. Far off in the kitchen, a radio had been turned on. Nite Hawk's voice concluding his program: *We wander, wonder. What is real, what is not?*

"So, you want to come back to my place? I could use some company. You too, right?"

"*It's what we have when we have nothing else*," she said, mimicking me, what I'd say whenever we were feeling this dead of night hopelessness together. "You're so easy to make fun of."

"Am I?"

"Yes."

"Jake the comedian with the mask of tragedy over his heart," I said.

"You know, if you didn't have at least that smidgen of self-awareness I'd ditch you as a paramour. There's hope for you, at least."

Back at my apartment, I didn't even try to make love to her—a situation we endured from time to time on our nights together.

Side by side we lay on the bed, a slant of moonlight falling across us. She had taken off her wig; her hair short, dark brown, cut close. Without her tight blouse and mini-skirt she was no longer a nostalgic fantasy. Simply Connie. A woman approaching forty, afraid of what was to come.

What she'd said about her life not changing, how things went on without a turning point, without resolution, was just as true for me. The thing, I believe, that bound the two of us together. Since Vera, the years had gone on and on, piling up, a heap of days and weeks without consequence. It was astounding—frightening really—how quickly the years pass, how easily life can slip through one's fingers.

"You never did tell me why you came by tonight, what's bothering you," she said.

"Old memories, is all."

"That woman? The one you were in love with?"

"Yes."

"You ever going to tell me about her, about what happened?"

"Maybe."

"When?"

"I don't know."

"*When?*"

"Some day."

"You see?" She propped her head up with one hand, her arm and elbow stabbing the mattress for support. "Some day. Some day. You're always pushing things off."

"Am I?"

"You're always telling me to deal with things, take action. If you want things to change, you've got *to make* a change. You tell me that every time I complain about something."

I squinted to see her eyes in the darkness. They were bright with a sudden fire. "So what's your point?"

"My point is you've been pushing this thing off your whole life."

I played dumb. "What thing?"

"This unresolved thing. This mystery woman you won't talk about. This woman you feel too guilty about to love anyone else. It's like she's there but she's not there."

"That's what ghosts are."

I was back in the cemetery, waiting to be forgiven for my sins and failures.

I reached up to stroke her cheek. "They're there and they're not there. It's what we have to live with."

35

Dreamtime.

A phone ringing.

Too loud. Too harsh.

Sound was the enemy. The stalker.

No escape. No refuge.

I jerked awake then. No one beside me. Sometime during the night, Connie had left without waking me.

The phone on the floor beside the bed. Jack Connelly's voice when I picked up.

"Guy I know in the Madison Houses, lower east side. Ex-con, owes me a favor." He waited till my grunt assured him I was listening. "Goes by the name of Marcos now. He thinks Monahan had something to do with his brother's death. Or maybe Blue Flower did. Says Monahan's tight with the crew that sells it. Just a hunch on my part. He might be able to help you connect the dots."

"Where do I find this guy?"

"He'll find *you*. Building 1408."

"When?"

"Tonight."

36

Till then, time to fill.

At the chapel near the cemetery, I found a priest in Franciscan robes dusting the marble altar. He was thin, stooped, his movements agonizingly slow. When he turned and noticed me, I saw how thin he really was, his small narrow face a collection of bones with the barest coating of flesh, his eyes staring out from deep sockets. When he spoke, his thin lips quivered. "Can I help you?"

I handed him the photo of Vera. "Can you tell me anything about this woman? She came here often in recent months."

The photo shook in his hand. Squinting, he held it at arm's length. The light through the stained glass was thin. Still, something in his clouded eyes let me know he recognized her. "May I ask why you're inquiring?"

"She's gone missing." I thought how I might make my appearance here sound legitimate. "I'm Jake Garrett, a friend, trying to help her husband locate her."

"Are the police involved?"

"Unfortunately they haven't been much help."

He took a step, teetering, seemed about to fall and I reached to take his arm, the child-like width of it. He settled on a wooden bench, thinking something over. "Your friend. She did come here from time to time. We spoke on several occasions. I don't think I'd be breaking any confidence to say she was unsettled. Grieving certainly for her lost child. And she appeared, to me at least, on the verge of something. Some decision she was deliberating."

He looked at me expectantly. "Could it be her disappearance was the result of that deliberation?"

"That's what I'd like to determine."

"I'll pray for her safe return." His frail shoulders trembled as he rose from the bench. "I believe she was a good woman. Struggling, like all of us, to find her way."

I felt the need to offer him something. "You meant a lot to her, I'm sure."

"She meant a lot to *me*. She was in need of kindness, the only thing I have left to give."

"Thank you, Father."

"One thing I do remember her saying." He looked down at the photo again. "It was a striking thing to say. I guess that's why it stuck in my mind."

He turned. His face, partly in shadow, partly in the window's dimmed light. "She said she wanted to get back to the source. To the land of fairy tales where she'd once been happy."

37

Several minutes past five. Waiting across the street from Sue's office. Following her as she walked part way down the block and hailed a cab. At the corner I stepped into a cab, told the driver to follow hers.

"No cops and robbers stuff for me," the cabbie said. "I don't do nothin' crazy."

"Just keep the cab in sight, if you can. That's all I'm asking."

He did a pretty good job of it, tailing her cab through the park and down Lexington to 59th. She got off at Bloomingdale's and, keeping my distance, I followed her in, watching as she made purchases: first at the cosmetics counter, then upstairs in lingerie.

On the street again she walked briskly toward Fifth, a woman with purpose, stopping at Saks where I watched her choose skirts and a blouse, and finally at Dolce & Gabbana where I stayed outside, the store too small for me to risk being noticed.

From there she walked west to the brownstone in Hell's Kitchen where she lived—Davison had given me the address along with her work address when I first went to see him.

Tenth Avenue in that area was well on its way to gentrification—new restaurants, upscale cafes, gourmet markets—but her street was still a mixed bag. A few un-renovated beaten-down tenements alongside expensive face-lifted brownstones like hers.

Her apartment was on the second floor, #2B. I resisted ringing her door bell. Instead walking down a side alley where, beyond a brick wall, I could see into the brownstone's back yard with its lone, stunted Mulberry tree. What I determined were her windows were both lit, visible above the gnarled branches of the tree.

I wondered if I was making a mistake not confronting her directly, demanding to know what the hell was going on; but I'd caught her in too many deceptions already to trust anything she might say. Better it seemed to keep her in my sights, let things play out as they would. At least a while longer.

In the alley's shadow, I took up my vigil. Reflecting on what little I knew about this woman with an interest in high-end fashion and low-end watering holes in the East Village.

Ten years back, when she was dating Monahan, she seemed as much a mystery as she was now. On the one hand: high-spirited, flirtatious, provocative not only in dress but in the innuendoes that shadowed even her seemingly innocent comments; on the other hand: that part of her that was dark and withdrawn, something hidden behind her smiles, a privacy she guarded with the ferocity of a junkyard dog. She rarely talked about herself, never about her past.

It was Vera's theory she had a deeply troubled childhood. After one of our dinner dates with Sue and Monahan, Vera told me the only thing she could remember Sue ever saying about her home life was that once, when she'd stayed out later than she was supposed to on her prom night, her father in a drunken rage shoved her head-first down the basement stairs and kept her locked there, bleeding on the stairs, till the next afternoon.

Which was a clue, Vera thought, why she was compulsively attracted to men like Monahan. When they were roommates in college, Vera said, Sue rarely went out with a decent, ordinary guy. After a date or two with one of them, she'd be bored, whatever. Mostly she was drawn to guys with an edge, angry guys, with unpredictable tempers. "At first I thought it was a masochistic thing, that she in a perverse way enjoyed being pushed around, treated badly. But after a while I began to wonder if *she* was really the one in control, if she was manipulating them in ways they didn't understand. That even she didn't understand."

Vera shrugged when she'd said it. "Only a theory. I really don't know. I've tried to convince her to stop seeing Mike but to no avail."

At the time I thought that each of them, in their own way, had a penchant for dangerous choices in romance. But I was in love. Which made it easy for me to forgive Vera for her infidelity. As long as I was the beneficiary of it.

Now I thought we were all victims of our inability to fully understand why we acted in the way we did. Which made it even more difficult to understand the actions of others. Sue, a particularly challenging case in point.

Which left me with nothing but my lonely surveillance—of her two illuminated windows behind which from time to time her figure passed, and the front entrance to her building.

No venturing out on her part. No visitors.

At ten o'clock, I called it quits.

Time to meet Marcos.

38

The bruised red-brick buildings of the Madison Houses, clustered around small areas of fenced-in grass and paved walkways, rose above the streets of Chinatown. Every fifty feet the darkness torn open by the garish yellow light of a sulphur lamp.

Bad idea going into the projects at night. But Connelly said Marcos didn't want to be seen in daylight talking to a white man. And he couldn't go far from his apartment, crippled as he was. The result of a shooting incident. His right foot had been torn up pretty bad.

We'd discussed talking to the police, now that there was some evidence Vera's disappearance might be more than a simple case of an unhappy housewife, but we didn't have enough yet to connect Monahan directly to the Blue Flower trade, and neither Connelly nor I thought we'd have much success getting the cops to go against one of their own, even if he was retired, simply on our hunch.

So there I was, alone, on a deserted walkway moving toward Building 1408.

At my approach a thin, brown-skinned scarecrow of a man leaning on a single crutch nodded at me from inside the entrance. On the wall behind him the spray-painted words, *Falsas Promesas.*

Large black dripping letters.

"Who made them? The false promises."

"Everybody." Marcos' voice was a rasp-like growl. His small hard face deep with wrinkles, making it hard to determine his age. "The city, the mayor, the housing authority that runs this place." He raised his hand to wipe something from his eye. The tattooed words BURY ME WITH SATAN on his arm. "And it don't only mean the busted toilets and elevators or the stink of piss in the halls. It means everything, the whole broke down dream."

He waved me toward the rear of the lobby. "Can't be standin' out here."

In the elevator—this was one of the few that *did* work, Marcos said—he leaned toward me. "Got somethin'?"

I handed him the hundred dollar bill I'd promised.

"Obliged," Marcos said. "Can't work no more 'cause a this foot a mine."

The elevator stopped at the tenth floor.

"Got to walk from here," he explained.

We were standing in a dimly lit hall. Apartment doors lining both sides. A barrage of sound: salsa, hip hop, R&B, voices raised in anger or laughter. A stairwell at the far end.

I pulled back. The stairwell was unlit.

"Can't get there no other way," Marcos said.

I held my ground a moment longer. So much easier, I was thinking, writing about crime than living in its world.

For Vera, I reminded myself.

Marcos' spectral, slumping form led the way up. The stairs pitch black. Grey light, a thin crease of it, beneath the door to the roof. Somewhere lower down, voices—and other sounds less identifiable—twisting upward. Bare cinderblock walls serving as echo chamber, intensifying the distortion. The stench of urine lifting from the darkness.

The stairwell door opened onto a narrow section of ground higher than, and walled off from, the main area of the roof. A waist-high brick ledge enclosed it. Beyond the ledge, the dark roofs of the project stretched away toward the river.

Leaning hard on his crutch, Marcos limped along the wall and stopped. "This be where it happened."

I waited but the man didn't explain. "Where what happened?"

"My brother. This be his grave. Here."

"I don't understand."

"His head be touching the wall right there, feet spread out that way. Hand over his heart like he needed somethin' to hold onto."

"Somebody killed him?"

"The Blue Flower. Stuff the crew here been sellin'. Brand new. Best a the best, what they say. So good you got to have it. So strong, some folks die. My bro, the first in Madison."

I leaned back against the wall for support. "You saw it happen? Your brother."

"No, sir. Somebody tole me. Find him here like I tole you." He shifted his weight on the crutch and lit a cigarette. "Wanna kill the crew that sells it, sure do. But cain't do no more time. Just cain't. Wanna do it, but cain't. Gonna die for sure, I go back in the joint."

He looked at me with dull, lightless eyes. "White dude comes lookin' for me. Finds me in the stairwell. Not doin' nuthin'. Sittin' there talkin' to this girl. He says he hears I'm tellin' stories. No sir, I say. Ain't tellin' nuthin'. He tells the girl, get lost. Just me and him then in the dark. Shoots me in the foot. The ankle. Shatters all my bones there, so I can't put weight on it no more. Then he laughs, tell me he don't want to hear no more stories."

"You go to the police?"

"So they can laugh at me, too? Got no witnesses, got nuthin'. Been in and outta Rikers three times. Been on and off the horse myself a few times. What they want to hear what I got to say?"

He shook his head in regret. "Besides, got them boys watchin' me. Think maybe not a good idea talkin' to you. But I wanna bring them down so bad. Think, you just some white boy don't look like a cop. Think, I needs the money. So here I am."

Marcos slumped against his crutch, his eyes turned inward. Weariness settling hard upon him. "'Sides," he said, "here in Madison you talk to the cops, you a dead man."

All of this seemed worlds away from the Vera I knew, but I showed him the photo of her and Sue and Monahan. "Recognize anyone here?" It seemed such an impossible leap to Vera, or to Sue in her crisply-tailored business attire, her self-assured manner. But then I never would have thought Vera would have succumbed to alcohol, either.

The door to the roof opened and I froze.

A teenage boy and girl came out, glanced in our direction warily before slipping away into darkness.

"Got to get their fun early," Marcos said. His eyes followed them with a forlorn, far-off look. "Come midnight the crew take over. Don't like no company."

He studied the photo in his hand. "Never seen these gals. But the dude. He the one shot my foot."

The roof door opened then, a second time.

A flash of light. An explosion of sharp, cracking sound from the stairwell's darkness. Marcos' crutch lifted and flew in the air. He lurched sideward, falling on me as I hit the ground.

I lay there afraid to move.

Breathing hard beneath his weight, his sudden stillness.

39

"Should never have sent you in there," Jack Connelly said on the phone the next morning. "What in hell's name was I thinking? What was I doing?" His breathing came through slow and heavy. "Sometimes I think they should just burn down all the projects, come up with some new plan to house the poor. Start again with a clean slate."

"*My* doing. *I'm* the one responsible for the old guy's death." A situation I would never have dreamed I'd find myself in. I was only a writer, after all, locked away in a room with a typewriter. Responsible only for the deaths of my characters. Then there I'd been—a scene all too real—on the roof of a housing project, standing over a dead man, waiting for the police to arrive.

I didn't know what to do with my guilt. In a weakened voice I said, "At least now we know for sure Monahan's dirty. But what I can't figure is, if he's making money off the drug trade, why's he live like he does. Like a pauper, 'cept for his Caddy."

"That's how dirty cops stay outta jail. Nothing too flashy. Probably's got an offshore account somewheres." A ruminative pause. "Whatever's going on must be some heavy shit. I'd walk away, I were you."

"Can't do that."

"'Course you can."

"Can't."

"We have choices, buddy. You're old enough to know that. We have choices. Most of the time, anyway."

"Not this time."

"She must be one hell of a woman." An exasperated sigh. "Or you're one hell of a fool."

"Both."

40

Guilt is a form of justice.

It needs no jury to convict, no locked cell.

Simply a man alone, face to face with an act he can't undo.

I was pacing the narrow confines of my apartment. Bookcase to bookcase, desk to bed, wall to wall. My mind pacing too, *racing*.

A voice was raised in my defense. *You couldn't have known.*

I should have known.

You were simply following a clue. What any detective would do.

Every act has its consequences.

But how can we foresee them, the consequences?

We own them whether we foresee them or not.

So we shouldn't act at all? For fear of what might happen?

I don't know. I don't know.

Can't you see how crazy that is? There'd be no such thing as life as we know it.

I caused a man to die.

It was for a greater good. To find Vera.

My greater good. Not his.

There are things beyond our control. You know that.

I caused a man to die.

You'll get past that. You'll find a way to forgive yourself.

And wasn't that, I thought, yet one more reason for our disquiet on this earth. We find a way to forgive ourselves for everything, no matter how serious the transgression.

At my desk, I stared at the typewriter I hadn't used in days. Then I began pacing again. It was just past 3 a.m. To escape the endless and restless traffic of my thoughts, I turned on the Nite Hawk. He was introducing a caller who referred to himself as Ditch Man, a poet of the streets whose coarse, muffled voice had a compelling authority. For all I knew he might have been one of the homeless men Vera and I had served at the Church of the Apostles.

"Look out east, west, high, low, what you hear? Nothing. *No thing*. Not even silence because, hey, silence is *some*thing. And what you hear ain't something, ain't anything. It's the hole inside the hole, the darkness inside you. What you gonna do? Can't tell top from bottom. Can't tell where you end and everythin' else begins. *You* the hole inside the hole.

"Always someone raggin' on me. Hey you, outta my way. Hey you, offa my cloud. Move it, buddy, move it. Don't sit here. Don't stand there. Keep movin'. Keep movin'. No sleeping here, no loitering, no smoking on the premises, no public displays of affection, no picnicking, no ball playing, no walking on the grass. Hey! Move it, shit-face. No farting, no sweating, no stinking up the place, no puking, no pissing, no public restrooms, no littering, no picture-taking, no eating, no drinking, no excuses, no *breathing*.

"How much a man got to hear 'fore he goes stone-deaf, 'fore his ear fall offa his head? Gonna quit this place. Gonna travel on—"

The man's rant ended: cut off abruptly, mid-sentence.

For a moment I stopped pacing.

I was reminded of a line I'd used in a recent novel: *And we, travelers blind of mind and spirit, follow the lonely road ahead.* But I liked this man's words better. *We're the hole inside the hole.*

41

I asked Davison about *the source,* the term the old priest said Vera used, but he had no idea what it meant.

We were at a playground near his house. Davison's idea. The basketball court, a game of one-on-one. "We need to stick together," he'd said on the phone, "in these troubled times." We were a team, as he saw it, and team members hung together, on-field as well as off.

But we'd been playing hard for twenty minutes and whatever comradery he'd expressed on the phone seemed to be dissipating quickly on the court. He came driving in for a lay-up, feinting left then right, then slamming into me before curling his body around me as he leapt to make the shot: a not-so-clean two points. It was the first time he charged directly into me, our bodies colliding with brute force, leaving me stunned at first and a little shaken.

In contrast to his everyday manner, on the court he was an aggressive son-of-a-bitch. He came at me again and again, each time it seemed with more force, greater intensity and determination. I tried to shrug it off, to attribute it to simple athletic competition but I could deceive myself only for so long. There was something brutally antagonistic and mean-spirited in the way he charged into me and I found myself responding in kind. Planting my feet firmly on the cement, tightening my arms, my chest, my shoulders in anticipation of his assault. Returning his force with a blunt force of my own. I was taking a perverse delight in facing off with him.

Despite having more than ten years on me, the man kept pounding the boards. His shirt off, his face and torso drenched in sweat, he came at me hard and fast and with such relentless energy it seemed he wanted to annihilate me on his way to making a shot. My feelings for him grew equally savage. I refused to give an inch when he came at me, my body taut with inflamed resistance as I pushed back against him.

He charged and dodged and charged again to make his lay-ups. There was no way he was going to lose. You could see that in his eyes, the rigid cast of shoulders. Like there was heavy money on the game.

A matter of life and death.

A jealous husband at long last enacting vengeance.

Finally it all came to a stand-off, a stand-still. Two immoveable objects facing one another. Heavy breathing. Heaving shoulders. Glaring eyes. I thought he might drop the ball and try to rip my head off. I welcomed it. I wanted the opportunity to beat him to a pulp.

But the moment passed.

He took a step backward and launched a jump shot that *whooshed* through the net.

Out of breath and reeling from the whirlwind belligerent pace at which we'd been playing, down by twenty points and little hope of making a comeback, I called it quits. "You're a different person on the court," I said, hoping to ease the tension.

"Am I?"

I wasn't sure if he was being coy. "You make it a blood sport."

"I play hard, I guess. My way of venting."

I stood beneath the back board, drying myself with a towel. Davison seemed content to let the late-afternoon air do the drying. In fact, he seemed to relish it, flexing his shoulders. If I didn't know his normally reserved self, I would have thought the man was showing off his trim chest and abdomen. No belly fat whatsoever. No love handles.

"It's the one thing I've kept up with," he was saying. "Exercise-wise. I come here three or four times a week, take shots, work on my lay-up. Maybe it's having a younger wife. More pressure to keep up, you know."

He might have meant that innocently enough but it felt to me like he was rubbing it in.

"How about you?" he was asking.

"B-ball's a thing of the past for me. Mostly I do weights, some biking, a hell of a lot of jogging and walking. Handball sometimes on a Saturday or Sunday."

The man seemed pleased with himself, pulling on his sport shirt slowly. He'd found something he was better at than I was. "The police are useless," he said. "I worry my heart out here, and they haven't come up with a thing."

"It's a big city. A lot's going on."

"So what more have *you* found? You haven't given me much so far."

"Not for want of trying."

"But still—"

Which I took to mean that I'd failed to live up to his expectations. Only later would I think that maybe this was the night he'd lost all faith in me, when he regretted placing his trust in me.

I repeated what I'd already told him. The priest's comment about the source. The photo of Sue and Vera and Monahan at the Blue Flower Bar. I said nothing about the possibility of heroin addiction or of Monahan's probable involvement with organized crime. Nor did I say anything about Marcos and my visit to the projects; he wouldn't have accepted that Vera had any connection to the underworld. And neither did I say anything about the extent to which my feelings for her had resurfaced, that I was far along the path of betraying him for a second time. But, as I said, he may have already sensed this.

He looked disappointed at what little I'd offered. "Why don't we grab a beer? Brainstorm a bit."

"Can't tonight. Things to do."

"Sure," Davison said. "I just thought—"

One look at the energy draining from his face explained it all. He was a middle-aged man at dusk, alone. Like me. Despite our conflicted past, despite the unbridgeable rift between us, we shared one thing in common this night: neither of us had someone to go home to.

Davison had pulled on his shirt and was pushing his hand through his hair to tame it. Around us, in fading light, the playground was emptying.

I patted his shoulder.

Which felt like a version of the Judas kiss.

I withdrew my hand quickly.

"Good game," I said.

42

That night, re-reading Vera's journal.

A call from Davison asking me to return the journal and her photographs. Something in the man's voice—impatience, yes, but something harsher and more demanding—taking me off-guard.

"Something wrong?"

"I've been thinking," he said. "I have a theory. I need everything back."

"Tomorrow. I can't come up there tonight."

"I can come down. Pick them up."

"Tomorrow will have to do," I told him.

He hung up, sounding frustrated. I half-expected he might show up at my door as he had that first night. From time to time I looked down at the courtyard, assuming I might see him there amid the shadows.

After midnight, I found what I was looking for. Two lines in Vera's journal that read: *There was a castle, a kingdom and a princess. My college years, drawn from the pages of a fairy tale.*

Which triggered my memory. Something she'd once said to me. How innocent and happy she'd been those years.

Before the cares of the world took hold.

43

Morning light flooding the porch of Davison's house.

He reached quickly for the journal and the envelope of photos. Forcefully, as if anticipating I would resist.

Downstairs, on the workbench, he spread out the photos, searching for something, snatching one here and there and setting it aside in a separate pile.

"This wall thing," he said. "It's in quite a few of the photos."

In some of the photos the couples *leaned* against a wall, using it as a support for their affectionate clinging to one another. In a few, they sat side by side *on* a wall.

"I thought it might be significant," Davison was saying. "I thought it might be a clue."

I said nothing about the Bow Bridge, the wall she had stood on and nearly fallen from. "I don't know. What do *you* think it means?"

Davison raised his hands, palms open, in uncertainty. "*You're* the detective. I thought it might trigger something."

"Some of my characters are detectives. I'm a writer."

"Same thing." His voice had a similar edge of impatience—resentment even—as when he'd asked for the photos back. "You knew her best," he said, his voice rising on the vicious thrust of an accusation.

"You knew her more recently," I countered, thinking *ten years of recent*, not bothering to hide my own rising resentment, my abiding jealousy.

"Do you recognize any of these walls? Where they might be?"

I stared again at the array of photos. In one, a boy and girl side by side stood on a wall, holding hands. In another, a dark-skinned boy and girl walked on a wall one behind the other as they teetered, struggling to maintain balance. And there was a photo of a girl about to jump or fall into her boyfriend's waiting arms. Again, I said nothing of the incident at Bow Bridge.

"I don't recognize where these were shot. Inwood Park maybe? The grounds of the Cloisters?"

"I haven't been to either place," he said.

I knew how, back then, Vera would have explained it. *Love's a balancing act between what we fear and what we desire.* It was a concept she'd expressed more than once, though whenever I pressed her on what those fears might be she would laugh it off and change the subject.

I said this to Davison whose shoulders slumped, his hands jammed sheepishly into his pockets. "It was foolish of me," he said, "to think you'd find anything tangible here."

Another accusation. He glared first at the photos, then at me, with equal disappointment. He began carefully gathering the photos and, together with the journal, put them into the desk drawer. It occurred to me that the questions about the wall might simply have been an excuse to take possession again of the photos and the journal, to get them out of my hands. His way of further distancing himself from me.

"I've been checking with the police two, three times a day," he said. "They're sick of me by now."

Upstairs the phone was ringing and he excused himself.

Which offered me the opportunity to look for the missing violent photos, their absence from the collection a continuing source of wonder.

The basement had been given a makeover. The floors had been swept and cleaned. The desk and work table had been tidied up. Nothing hanging from the wire.

I checked the cabinets beneath the table and the desk drawers. No hidden stack, no buried collection. Whatever Davison had done with those particular photos, they were nowhere to be found in the basement.

What I did find, though, in the bottom drawer of a desk pushed against the back wall, a desk piled high with notebooks, thesis binders and student science papers, was a handgun. It was far back in the drawer. A Baretta M9.

My first instinct was to take it, get it out of the house, out of Davison's hands; but I left it there surrounded by index cards and paper clips. It might have been there for some time. It might have nothing to do with Vera's disappearance.

Once more, to my way of thinking, it seemed a better plan to let things play out as they would. A decision I hoped I wouldn't later regret.

I climbed the stairs and stood in the living room, amid the hundreds of trinkets and mementoes Vera had collected.

Instead of jealousy, this time I felt a kind of pity for Davison and a more general feeling I couldn't explain—of sadness for us all: Davison, Vera, myself.

Davison came from the kitchen where he'd finished his call. He looked at me with a wary concern. "You'd tell me if you've found something, wouldn't you? You're not hiding anything from me, are you?"

I worded my response carefully to avoid a lie. "I haven't located her, if that's what you're asking."

What I said next was a promise I hoped I could keep. "If I find her, you'll be the first to know."

44

Two men, a black Lincoln Town car.

Outside Davison's house, the car sitting in the shade of a tree farther down the street.

I thought nothing of it till, five blocks later, I was climbing the steps of the el. There it was again, parked on the far side of the street. Whoever they were, they knew my route home.

But I wasn't on my way home just then.

Instead I took the train *uptown* to the next stop. A short walk to Mercycrest, the college Vera had attended. Perched on a hill. A lawn running down to the Hudson. At the hill's crest, a castle-like building. A massive façade of grey stone, turrets, arched windows, oaken doors. In front of it a garden of shrubs and flowers, a fountain in its center.

A castle, a kingdom, a princess, Vera's journal entry had read.

Classes were over for the summer, few students around, but I did find a janitor on a smoke-break outside the castle who, after studying the photo, said that he might have seen her. "Maybe her," he said.

"When?"

"Couple, few days. Takes long walk by the river. Sits in garden. Many children with her."

"Children?"

"Yes."

I gave the man my card. If he saw her again.

On my street in the Village, the black Town car with what looked like the same two men inside was parked not far from the alley.

Turning abruptly I skirted the block, came around to the

building behind mine where the lobby door was always open, took the stairs.

Every paranoid crime writer has an escape route.

Easy enough jump from roof to roof—*if* you didn't look down before you made the leap. I took the stairs down to my apartment, kept the lights off.

Sue Quinn's call came in the dark. She'd heard from Vera, she said. Vera wanted to meet me later that night.

A moment of pure adrenaline before the assault of questions and doubts. "Is she all right?"

"Yes. Yes. She's fine."

"Where is she? What's she been doing?"

"She said she'd explain everything."

"Where? When?"

"The West 72nd Street entrance to the park. At eleven. I'll meet you there."

"She's been living in the park?"

Sue's laugh was short and tight. "She wants to meet there, that's all. She said you'll know why. She wants you to come alone, without Norm."

"Why all this secrecy?"

"You'll have to ask *her*."

I had a hard time tempering my impatience. "That's all you're going to tell me?"

"That's the way she wants it," Sue said.

45

As promised, shortly before eleven, Sue was waiting at the West 72nd Street entrance. Tight jeans, a man's grey windbreaker unzipped enough to make it appear she had no shirt on underneath. Other than that, no effort to dazzle me with her womanly charms. Instead she offered a brief, business-woman smile before leading me briskly along the park drive, heavy with shadow and closed to vehicular traffic. She kept her eyes averted, clearly not interested in conversation.

When I joked about the cloak and dagger nature of this venture, she said, "Yes, it was, wasn't it," in a way that suggested she didn't find the comparison amusing. In response to questions about what Vera said or didn't say in Sue's conversation with her, Sue said, "I can't say any more than I have. I'm sorry."

"You haven't exactly been up front with me, have you?"

She gave me a quick, nervous glance. "About this?"

"About everything."

"I don't know what you mean," she said, hurrying on.

This time of night Bethesda Terrace had a lonely, desolate feel. A few people sat around the fountain rim. The splashing water a hollow, empty sound in the darkness. When Sue turned onto the northwesterly path along the lake, I knew where we were heading.

"Vera's bridge," I said.

Sue nodded. "She said you'd know the significance."

"One of our special places."

"She told me that, yes."

I tried to press her. "What else did she say?"

Sue, walking a step or two ahead, ignored the question.

The walkway was dark, only an occasional street lamp. When the bridge came into view I could make out the figure of a woman standing at its center, her slim, dark form turned away from us, facing the water. My breath came faster, my step quickened.

Beside me, Sue's pace had slowed. She whispered, "Be careful, Jake. Run if you can."

She turned away, swallowed quickly by the heavy leaf-shadow of the dirt path she had veered onto.

I hesitated only a moment. Vera was no more than fifty feet ahead, her back to me, standing at the highest point on the arch of the bridge, silhouetted against the lake. Behind her, the buildings of Central Park West rose above the tree line. Then she was moving away from me toward the far end of the bridge.

I began to run, calling her name, but she was walking quickly, off the bridge now, turning onto a path into the trees. For one brief second she turned and I saw that it wasn't Vera at all but a woman with the same body type, the same dark hair.

An expressionless white face.

A stranger.

Then she was gone, lost in the shadow of the trees.

Emerging from that same darkness were two men, masked: a thin white man and a larger, muscular dark-skinned man.

Footsteps behind me. Two more men on the bridge, coming toward me.

Sue's whispered words, *Run if you can,* echoing in my ears.

Then they were on me. Pinning my arms back. Offering me up for sacrifice.

The white man's rasp of a voice said, "This is what you get asking the wrong people the wrong questions." He swung at my face first then at my mid-section, knocking the air out of me. He swung again and again, the pain splitting me apart, or so it felt, waist to toes. "Keep nosing around, believe me—it's gonna be worse."

Falling under the weight of the blows, I thought—beyond the edges of pain—of Vera, wondering yet again how this could have anything to do with the woman I loved.

46

Advil. A shower.

Keeping the lights off in my apartment.

Assessing the damage, by flashlight.

I felt sure the building was still being watched.

My head, shoulders, and belly throbbed with soreness more than pain. Bruises had formed, especially around my mid-section, and I felt nauseated. Once I'd cleaned the blood from my lips, though, my face didn't look too bad. The upper lip was swollen and a bruise discolored a section of forehead close to the hairline. If I brushed my hair forward, the discoloration was partly covered, particularly to a casual observer.

In the dark I stood at the window, looking down at the courtyard with its now fully blossoming trees, its permanent shadows tucked into the corners where the buildings abutted one another, its thin flicking shadows thrown by the fountain's spray.

At the courtyard's edge, another shadow.

At the tip of the alley.

I blinked to clear my vision. Shadows hid everything except the lower portion of a pair of pants above a man's shoes. The figure was close enough to the courtyard, the shoes set at such an angle, to suggest whoever it was had a full view of my building, the window at which I stood.

Shadows shifted, revealing more of the dark figure: legs, a partial torso. The face, though, still obscured.

Several minutes passed. The man remained, nearly motionless, save for the occasional shifting of his feet.

I called Sue. Her answering machine picked up.

No surprise.

I slipped out through the escape route and took a cab to Hell's Kitchen. Down the side alley to check her windows. Dark, as I expected. Windows closed. Curtains drawn. The back yard silent, empty. The leaves of the Mulberry tree lifting in the breeze.

I paced the alley, end to end, fury pounding at my temples like the pressure of a migraine.

A hopeless gesture, but I pressed her front door button. Holding my finger on it in rage, for more than a minute. Hearing in my mind that hollow sound a buzzer makes in an empty apartment. Or was she in the shadows there, holding her breath, keeping still, so as not to give herself away?

It wasn't only the betrayal and beating I couldn't forgive. It was that extra added touch of perversity. After all, she could have taken me to any deserted area of the city. But to use the Bow Bridge, to make me believe that Vera was within reach after all this time, all these years—that, I felt, was beyond unconscionable.

I slammed my hand against the buzzer, then the flat of my fist, again and again. Through the intercom an agitated voice from one of the other apartments shouted, "Who is it? Who is it? What's the matter? What's going on down there?"

Another voice, equally agitated, joined in: "I'm calling the police. Right now. Right this minute."

As I turned away I was thinking of Vera's comment about Sue's choice in men. *Men with an edge. Angry men with unpredictable tempers.*

I had to laugh—bitterly, to be sure.

I was one of them, wasn't I?

For surely, on more than one occasion, she'd offered herself to me. Unless that, too, was another of her deceptions.

You have to step outside yourself to see yourself. This was one of those times. Who was this guy, blind with both love *and* hate, descending the stairs to the street, head bent low and shoulders hunched tight around his inner darkness, hurrying toward Tenth Avenue?

I fell squarely into the profile. Someone who didn't fit in anywhere, a loner, angry at what I'd lost, what I thought life was withholding from me.

The voice again, insisting on the truth I still found ways to ignore.

*What **you** lost. What **you** withheld from yourself.*

47

The Neon Angel.

The Belle Tones finishing up their last set with a rendition of *Please, Mr. Postman*, Connie singing lead, Pixie and Dixie doing back-up. With their mini-skirts and cute little girl-group dance steps they were thrilling the decent-sized crowd, baby boomers for the most part, in their fifties, clapping and swaying in their seats. A few had gotten up to dance, hesitantly at first, rusty.

The vibe here, always upbeat and positive, lifted my spirit despite the night's events, my aching body. The place was a den of nostalgia: not only the music but the décor itself, the walls papered with posters of the Crystals, the Marvelettes, the Shirelles, the Chantels, the Angels, the Shangri-Las, the Ronettes, Martha and the Vandellas. 45 RPMs and album covers from the days of vinyl hung as ornaments over the bar. It was a world that existed in my childhood and it still fascinated me. Maybe because I simply liked the music.

"Nostalgia's another name for selective memory," I said to Connie when the set ended. "You remember only the good times. It simplifies the past by revealing so little of it."

"You mean like the reality of you and that woman? The one you loved?"

I wanted to say, 'No, not like that. What I felt for her, *feel* for her, is real. It's love, not nostalgia. I know the difference.' What I *did* say, lamely, because I couldn't take anymore conflict this night was, "Everything has to be tested."

"How are you going to do that?"

I didn't have the heart, not this night, to fill her in about what had transpired these past days, the steps I was taking in hopes of one day being able to prove my love. So I said nothing.

When I turned, my face caught the light above the bar.

"What happened to you?" she asked with alarm.

"Long story," was all I said.

At the diner a few minutes later, Alphonse brought us coffee. He noticed my face but was gracious enough not to ask about it.

When we were alone, Connie said, "So you going to tell me what happened?"

"You'll read about it someday. In one of my books."

"You know," she said, "You're a hard man to have a relationship with. Even a friendship."

"I know. I'm sorry."

And I was. I just didn't think I could change that right now.

She played with her cup, tilting it on the saucer, tentative when she asked if I wanted her to come over.

"Tonight's not good." I couldn't quite imagine her jumping from rooftop to rooftop in the dark.

What I said was also the truth. "I hurt too much." To ease the disappointment she couldn't quickly enough or completely enough mask, I added, "I'll make it up to you. I promise."

"When?"

But I was already lost in the unanswered questions of the night.

48

In my apartment, lights off, considering my options.

Ditch Man talking once again on the Nite Hawk show:

". . . Been on the move. 'Ricans lookin' at me funny from their stoops, Koreans givin' me the evil eye I go near their fruit stand, yuppies pretendin' not to see my open hand when they're buying their thirty dollar bottles a Merlot. Don't want no Merlot. Just a cup a coffee.

"Knock on the door: Good Samaritan Parish. Friar Tuck tells me soup kitchen's closed.

"Don't want no soup, don't need no kitchen. Just some coffee, Father, please.

"Looks me up n' down like I was applyin' for work, like I asked him to diddle my pole. 'One cup,' he says, 'then on your way.'

"Can I use your bathroom, Father, while I'm here?

"'Restrooms for the clergy only,' says he. Pours me half a cup, real slow, like it's blood he's donatin'. 'On your way,' he says.

"What, no sugar?

"'Already put it in,' he says, 'one cube.'

"One cube ain't nothin', man. Need me six or seven, minimum. Got me a trip to take.

"'Piss off before you piss me off,' he says and shows me the door. No goodbye, no 'Hey buddy, good luck.' No 'Come back 'n' see us next time you're in the hood . . .'

"Up Broadway got to piss so bad got tears in my eyes. Look out west, what you see? Sadness fallin' with the dark. But man got to rise above. So he pray to God. Help me, help me, help me. Gimme shelter. Gimme a warm body to lie next to. God says, 'All right, good for you, now you gonna find me and I'm gonna show you the way. Here's how it works. Each time I take somethin' from you, you're gonna be one step closer to me.'

"I says, 'Lord, they done already take everythin' I got. Ain't nothin' left to lose.'

"And the Lord, he just throw back his big bald head and laugh and laugh and laugh. . . ."

A moment passed before Nite Hawk's voice filled the dead air space: "Hang in there, Ditch Man. Hang on tight." Then he added, "There's a little bit of the Ditch Man in all of us. Isn't there?"

My mind adrift.

Thinking how relative our discontents are.

Thinking that Vera would have gotten a kick out of the homeless man's interchange with the Almighty. At least the Vera I once knew.

Thinking it was time to make my next move.

I checked the courtyard. The figure in the alley was still there, revealing enough of himself—it now seemed intentional—to assure I knew I was under surveillance.

I packed a few necessities in an overnight bag and left my apartment by way of the escape route.

49

I checked into a motel wedged between a public housing project on the Yonkers border and a McDonald's in the Bronx, three blocks from the Mercycrest campus. A rough neighborhood, run-down and poor.

I spent the day on campus, showing Vera's photo to anyone I came across. The janitor I'd spoken to last time was nowhere to be found. But mid-afternoon, at Cupid's fountain in the garden, I came upon Sister Anne, a young woman who looked to be still in her teens. She seemed flustered when I sat on the bench beside her. Her face reddening. Her hand going quickly to her mouth when I showed her Vera's picture.

"Oh," she said, her voice a soft tremble.

"Does that mean you've seen her?"

"I can't say." Her head piece left exposed the pale skin of her face, her wide curious brown eyes.

"Can't or won't?"

She gathered her long robe and stood abruptly. "You'll have to speak to Mother Superior," she said, turning away.

"Where can I find her?"

"I don't know." She stopped then in her retreat, looking guilty or perhaps fearful that she'd told, if not a lie, then a partial truth. "She's away at a conference."

"When will she be back?"

"Tomorrow. I think."

With small quick steps, her face still flushed, she hurried across the garden.

Leaving me with the endlessly bubbling fountain. The cherub as was his custom in his perpetually exultant mood, spouting a thin hard stream of water from pursed lips, his arms extended, legs thrust backward and upward so that it appeared he was suspended in air, mid-flight. Unburdened by sorrows of the flesh.

50

Evening.

Lights shining through the curtains of every room in the motel but the one next to mine. R&B thumping loudly from that darkness.

Inside, the walls of my room shook. My image, dimmed and receding in the mirror, stared back. A face, with its bruised forehead, more drawn than normal: too old for its years. I appeared—I searched for the word to describe myself—*incomplete*. A face that was lacking something. An absence of—of *what*?—something necessary in the eyes. I wondered if it had ever been there, that necessary thing, or if I'd lost it along the way. Once again Davison's words came to me: *You're the key.*

I turned them around: *she's* the key. *Vera is the key.*

I listened to Sue's recorded phone message again. When I called the Manor her boss, Carlos, said she was out of town. I told him who I was, that Sue's friend, Vera, had disappeared. That I was concerned for both of their safety.

"She's on vacation," he said.

"How long?"

"Two weeks. Maybe three."

"Where?"

"You know Sue. Her private life's a secret. Always has been."

I thought of a line one of my characters spouted in a recent novel: *Our secrets define us.*

"It's crucial I get in touch with her," I persisted, hoping he might offer me something more. "Under the circumstances, I'd say it's a matter of life and death."

"Wish I could help. Really do."

"In the past. Her vacations. She ever mention where she went?"

Carlos' slow breathing filled the wires. "Yeah, once in awhile she'd talk about a trip. The islands mostly. Jamaica, the Bahamas, St. Croix. Once she went to Haiti. But those were all winter trips. This is the first time she's gone away in summer."

"Those trips. You know who she went with?"

"By herself, I think. 'Least she never mentioned anyone. My hunch is she liked the uncertainty. Who she might meet along the way. What might happen. That sort of thing, you know. A walk on the wild side." He laughed at something. "Asked her to go away with me a few times. Hey, a guy's got to try, right? She wanted nothing to do with that. A kick in the nuts, for sure. And I'm the type of guy who don't take rejection easy. But she was too good a businesswoman to let go."

"How about friends, acquaintances, in the city?"

Again, his slow breathing. "She was close to that woman you mentioned, Vera. I would overhear them sometimes, on the phone."

"Did you catch anything, I mean especially their recent calls, anything you overheard?"

"Nah, not really."

"What about the men in her life? She ever mention anybody?"

"Not by name. There was someone she talked to from time to time. On the phone. Quick calls, mostly. No more than a minute or so. Never said who." He was silent a moment before saying, "For awhile there, I even thought she might be a lesbo. You never know, right? Anything's possible."

"If you think of anything that might help locate her—"

"If I hear from her, I'll let you know. You too, okay?"

"Of course."

He exhaled, a long slow sigh as if he was thinking something over. "I thought it was just Sue being Sue. Now you got *me* worried."

51

Sore body, sore mind.

On the bed I stared at the water-stained ceiling thinking about the phrase, *Sue being Sue*. Wondering what that meant when you knew so little about a person. Had I missed something—a word or a phrase, something she said or did—that might lead me to her?

I lay there pondering that. Then the mundane world inserted itself, as was its habit, into the midst of even the gravest of situations. I was hungry. I wondered where, other than McDonald's, I might go for dinner.

The music next door had abruptly been turned off. In its wake a commotion of excited voices, male and female, and then the voices, too, abruptly cut off. An outside door slammed, a forceful pounding on my own door. When I pulled it open, a thin fidgety man greeted me. Rust-colored skin. Wide smile. Yellow teeth.

"Name's Reynaldo," he said. "We be neighbors. Wondrin' could you do me this favor, be a small one." He held a paper bag in his hand and he raised it waist high. "Need you to keep this a few minutes, that's all."

"What is it?"

"Nothin'. Ain't nothin'." The man's shoulders twitched and he shifted his feet. His body shifting too, loose and elastic. His hand unsteady as he thrust the bag at me. "Nothin'. Jus' keep it for me."

When I made no move to take it, he dropped to a crouch and slid the bag into the space between my legs and the door frame. Then he was moving away, back to his room, mumbling, "Thanks, man. Sure do thank you a heap."

Taken aback, I watched him disappear behind the door of his room. The silence of the parking lot broken by the low beat of salsa somewhere on the courtyard's far side. I pushed the door closed and bent to pick up the bag which had made it halfway to the bed.

A pistol inside.

A .38. A Saturday night special.

Once I'd used one at a shooting range, doing research for a book.

I checked the chamber. Loaded.

Before I had time to decide what to do with it, the parking lot erupted with police lights and sirens. I shoved the gun back into the bag, shoved the bag itself under the bed and turned out the lights. Through the blinds, I watched a half dozen patrol cars one after the other come hurtling into the lot, officers taking up firing positions behind them while four of their own moved in my direction.

The room next door turned out to be the object of their assault. Within moments, the man who had called himself Reynaldo was being led out, hands cuffed behind him, head bowed as he was pushed into the back of a cruiser. Two women, also cuffed, wearing halter tops and short skirts, were brought out after him and forced into a second cruiser.

So it was obvious why he had to get rid of the gun. I already knew why he'd passed it off to me rather than simply chucking it out the bathroom window into the alley behind. Those windows were sealed shut; I'd tried to open mine earlier to circulate the air.

Within minutes, the cruisers and their flashing lights were gone, leaving the lot in an eerie silence. No one ventured out in the aftermath of the siege.

I double-locked the door, decided I wasn't hungry, after all.

52

The room hot, airless. I couldn't sleep.

My fortieth birthday. A fact obscured by the day's activities. Another of life's milestones thrown at me like a taunt.

For a while in the dark I listened to the radio. One show following another until Nite Hawk came on. The man's opening words as familiar as a phone call from a friend in the wee small hours:

NEW YORK CITY, 3 A.M.

What do we do with the night?

We sleep.

We dream . . .

The caller was Eva, a sixty-year-old woman, who spent her nights at a neighborhood bar where her man walked out on her nearly two years before. They'd had so many good times there she just couldn't stay away. "I come here hoping Walter might show up again some night," she said. "In the rain, most likely. That would be *so* like him, walkin' in out of the rain, no coat, no hat, his hair slicked back." Then she was defending herself, saying, "I know I know, nowadays a woman ain't supposed to be hangin' on a man, waitin' for him to get good and ready to come find her. A woman's got to be what they call pro-active. Go out and make her mark on the world, and all that. But you think it's easy, comin' here waiting on Walter like this? Hell, it takes effort and perseverance. It takes *commitment*, something this world could use a lot more of. How many times do I want to give up, stay home, drink myself numb, say to hell with everything, fall all the way down, deeper than any ditch. Hey, I *am* pro-active. Drag myself out of bed every damn morning, put in a full day's work, eat right to keep my figure, haul myself out here to the Paradise Bar & Grill night after night, just so's I'm ready for Walter when he comes—"

But it was my own story that consumed me.

My rather ordinary childhood in a housing development of bland brick buildings in the Bronx. How I tried to make my life more thrilling by reading mystery and adventure stories—about explorers, cowboys, seafarers, pirates, buried treasure. How I would venture to more dangerous neighborhoods, sometimes at night, to explore dark streets, back alleys, anything that involved a risk. A little bit of fear gave the game more edge. And how, above all, I wanted a life different from and more exciting than my parents'.

Well, I guess I got it.

One night, I thought, I might be one of Nite Hawk's callers, telling my tale of things lost and broken. If I lived long enough. If the beating I'd suffered wasn't prelude to something worse.

At least I could say this about myself on the eve of my fourth decade on this planet: like Eva waiting night after night for her man to return, my resolve would not weaken. My need to find Vera would prevail.

And that, in turn, led me to *her* need. The need—it seemed to me at this hour—of us all. Getting back to the place where we'd once been happy.

The land of fairy tales.

The source.

53

In the morning, I decided I should simply leave the gun where it was, under the bed. Who knew what it had been used for, what crimes had been committed with it? With a bathroom towel, I wiped it clean and slid it back under the bed. Let the cleaning lady find it, do with it what she would.

I walked as far as the street before turning back. Unlocking the door, closing it behind me, leaning against it. Dust floating in the motes of sunlight from the window. I closed my eyes and thought hard.

You don't need it.

But I might.

You're not a violent man.

How can you be sure?

Your life thus far.

Past performance is no guarantee of future results.

We're not talking about the stock market here.

Who can predict human nature?

You're a writer, not a killer.

I write about killers, don't I?

That doesn't make you one.

I could write about anything but I chose crime, violence.

Your characters commit acts of violence. Not you.

I created them, didn't I? I give them life.

Fiction isn't real life. You of all people should know that.

Writers write about what they know, what's inside of them.

Thoughts are not actions.

Thoughts precede actions.

All the more reason then to leave it here.

But—

I knelt down and pulled the bag from under the bed. I

removed the gun from the bag, hand around the grip, holding it to the window light.

Violence begets violence.

Yes.

So leave it.

What if I need it? Self-defense. What if I need it to save Vera?

You'll use your wits. Your smarts.

You give me too much credit.

If you get caught with it, you could face criminal charges: accessory to murder, obstruction of justice. Leave it. Leave it here.

I wiped the gun clean again, this time with my sleeve, placed it back in the bag, pushed it under the bed.

Smart move.

I turned to leave again, hand on the door.

At the last minute, though, I stepped back, reached under the bed and stuffed the .38 into my overnight bag.

It wouldn't be the last time I acted against my better judgment.

54

Inside the castle, the reception desk was unattended. From deep in the bowels of the building came the murmur of women's voices.

An elderly nun appeared at the end of the hall, hurrying toward me. "I'm so sorry," she said, nearing the desk. "I was called away for a moment." In response to my request to see the Mother Superior, I was told she was expected within the hour. "Our schedules are not quite so rigid, you see, during the summer months."

I showed her the photo of Vera. The nun's face went from welcoming to stony. "I see," she said, tight-lipped. "You'll have to wait for Mother."

I was granted permission to wait in the east reception room with its sparkling chandeliers and Victorian-era furniture, the walls hung with portraits of stately women in elegant, floor-length evening gowns.

An hour passed before the elderly nun came in to announce that Sister Dolorita, our dear Mother Superior, would see me now.

Her office was on the far side of the ballroom. A room with a single narrow leaded-glass window that did little to brighten the atmosphere, or her mood. From behind her massive desk, her middle-aged face was sallow in color, her pinpoint eyes examining me through round, rimless glasses. Not a cordial examination. "So you're the one who's been making inquiries."

"Yes, I—" I explained that Vera had attended college here, that we'd been very close and that I regretted having lost contact with her. She'd gone missing, there was a chance she was in danger—*et cetera*, *et cetera*.

Sister Dolorita's expression, if anything, hardened. "It seems to me, if I may be so bold, this is some kind of guilt thing on your part, is it not? You think you've failed her in some way, and this, this quest of yours is your way of making amends, some kind of hoped-for second chance."

She leaned toward me. The pinpoint knots of her eyes tightening even more. "Have you considered the fact that some things can't be undone, that living with our regrets is the punishment God has levied upon us?"

"I'm simply asking if you've seen her lately, if she's been here, on campus. Can you at least confirm that for me?"

Sister Dolorita sat stolidly behind the desk, her stare unblinking. "I will neither confirm nor deny such a thing. As a matter of policy we do not release information about our students, current *or* former."

As I was leaving, she said, "May I remind you, sir, this is a private college. Our grounds are private property and are not open to the public."

"I appreciate the reminder, Sister. To my long list of transgressions, I'll be sure to add trespassing."

Moments later, as I was crossing the garden, I felt sure that Vera had come back to the good sisters of the Sacred Heart, and they had become the guardians of her secrets.

A voice was calling behind me, "Sir. Sir?"

Sister Anne came toward me, half-running, one hand clutched to her side to raise her long gown above her ankles to keep from tripping. She stopped, red-faced and breathless, glancing quickly over her shoulder at the castle before saying, "She was so good with the children."

"What children? Who?"

"The woman you're seeking."

"Vera?"

"Yes, Vera." She said the name with a hushed reverence.

"She's here?'

"She *was* here." She drew a breath, tried to steady herself. "She helped with our summer children's program. She was wonderful, in the true meaning of the word. She was a wonder, full of wonder. The children loved her and she was an inspiration to me."

Sister Anne's eyes were aglow. She searched for the exact words she wanted. "Her heart was broken, she told me she had nothing left to give, but she gave the children so much. She gave all of herself. That, I believe, is the true meaning of love: to give when you have nothing left to give." She blushed self-consciously. "It's what I myself aspire to, though I fear without the grace of God I shall never reach my goal."

"Tell me, Sister, where is she now?"

"I don't know."

I studied her face, searching out the lie.

"It's true," she said. "None of us knows. Not even Mother Superior. She told us only that she had to begin a new life. Then one morning she was gone."

"When was that?"

"Two days ago."

I considered that. Vera's second disappearance—from here—coincided with Sue's vanishing act. It seemed likely, or at least possible, there was a connection.

"Has she stayed here before?"

"Yes. But never for so long." She lowered her eyes in shame. "Mother Superior would never forgive me for telling you. She considers the campus a sanctuary for our graduates in need. But you seem so troubled. I thought you should know." She hesitated, fumbling it seemed to justify her actions. "My instincts tell me you're a good man."

"Thank you, Sister."

"Do you think it's wrong to follow an instinct when it departs from—from what's expected of you by your superiors?"

"I'm glad you did." Then, because she was clearly hoping for greater reassurance than that, I added, "In this instance, I'm sure you did the right thing."

She glanced again uncertainly at the castle. "I'll pray that I did."

When I left the campus a few minutes later, I checked the street for anyone lurking. No Lincoln Town car. No one loitering suspiciously outside the college gate.

Whoever was watching me, hadn't yet found me here.

55

Vera's voice filled the small, dark space of my apartment.

"I've been on a journey," she said, "a journey that's still in progress. Even now, this moment, as I speak. I started out in happiness but ended in tears, though I'm hopeful still. I'm nurturing hope like an unborn child. Along the way, on my journey, I've learned so much, but of all those things *this*, I think, is most important of all: Love, like trust, must be earned."

A long, quiet moment followed.

It was Nite Hawk's voice I heard next, saying, "Thank you, Vera. From somewhere deep in the heart of the American night." Then he repeated her words: "*Love, like trust, must be earned*." A half-beat of silence intervened again before he added, "Wisdom in the dark hours."

Stunned, I sat at my desk. Her voice still filling the room, or so it seemed. What to make of it—her showing up like that? I wanted to believe it was me, and not Davison, she was reaching out to. And though above all I was relieved to know she was apparently safe and free from danger, I couldn't erase the enduring anger and disappointment I felt that she didn't contact me directly. Did I mean so little to her now? Could I have meant so little to her then?

Through the window I watched the figure in the alley. Same shadowed view: legs, shoes. A man of medium build from what I could tell. He'd been there since nightfall. I couldn't determine if he was the same person who'd been there two days before. Or whether he was one of the two men in the black Lincoln Town car.

Frustrated, I paced in my cell. Trapped there in the dark since my return from the campus. Dead end, it seemed, at every turn. I kept the radio on, half-expecting to hear Vera's voice again.

Finally, I took the .38 from my overnight bag.

In the courtyard I moved slowly but with determination toward the opening of the alley. Holding the gun at my side. Hoping I wouldn't be seen by my neighbors.

No movement, no sign of the figure who'd been standing there. I walked to the street where I saw no one. Nothing but a cat rubbing itself against the brick façade of the corner restaurant, dark now, as still and melancholic as the row of parked cars and the heavy, leaf-filled branches of the plane trees.

Heart pounding, I stood there breathing heavily.

Making my way back through the alley, crossing the courtyard, I kept glancing behind me.

Within minutes the phone rang.

My first thought was that it had to be one of the men following me. A campaign of harassment, intimidation. The menace of an anonymous call.

But it was a woman's voice.

She was so sorry for what happened, Sue said. She hadn't had a choice. But she wanted to make it up to me.

I listened without saying anything.

"Vera," she said. "She's in South Carolina."

"Why? What's she doing there?"

"I can't go into it on the phone." She took a breath before adding, "She doesn't know I'm calling you. But I'm doing this for her, too. I know she wants to see you, though she's too afraid or stubborn or proud or whatever to admit it."

"Where? Where in South Carolina?"

"The Hidden Nook Cabins. Near Hilton Head."

I knew the place. Had stayed there years before with Vera. Stolen days when Davison was away. A trip we'd jokingly called our honeymoon. Was it that memory that brought her back there? The good times we'd lost?

I wanted to believe it was. It couldn't simply be coincidence.

Or was this another of Sue's deceptions?

"Why did you set me up for that beating?"

"I told you. I didn't have a choice. I'll explain everything when I see you."

"How do I know you're not setting me up again?"

"I'm not, Jake. I swear it."

"Put her on the phone. Let me hear her voice."

"I can't do that."

"Why not?"

"I told you. She doesn't know I'm calling. I'm not with her right now."

"Where are you?"

"South Carolina, I told you. We're both here."

"Why should I believe you? Why should I believe any of this?"

"Because you don't have a choice." She let a silence fall between us. "Not if you want to see Vera again."

56

Pixie and Dixie were leaving the diner, each giving me a kiss on their way out, waving back to me through the window once they were on the street. I slid into the booth facing Connie. She was still in costume.

The diner was crowded this time on a weekend night. A raucous handful of the Bridge-and-Tunnel crowd laughing and talking over one another at a table near the door. I ordered an espresso from Alphonse, then leaned closer to Connie, forcing a smile. "There are things I have to tell you. Things I should have told you before but couldn't. I didn't have the words. I didn't understand it enough myself to explain it."

"About the ghost woman?"

"She's not so ghostly now."

"Oh," Connie said, her face suddenly still.

"She's come back into my life."

"Does she have a name, this woman?"

It took me a moment to say, "Vera."

"See? That wasn't so hard, was it?"

I deserved the mockery, for my reticence, my close-fisted reluctance to reveal any of this before. I bowed my head in acknowledgement, spoke softly, beginning with Vera's disappearance, concluding with the phone call from Sue. "I have to go to her," I said.

"Of course you do."

I studied her to see if she was mocking me again but what I saw in her face was far from sarcasm. Not so much resignation, as a recognition, an affirmation of what she'd known one day she would have to face. I said, "I'm sorry."

"For being true to yourself? No one should have to apologize for that."

But I felt further explanation was needed. For myself, as

well as for her. "I've learned a few things," I said. "It's taken me a long time, much longer than it should have." Her eyes were wet now. She pulled away her hand when I reached for it.

"It's all right," she said. "I'm a big girl."

So I forged on with my explanation. "It all seemed so much a mystery to me, what it was that made our love fail, Vera and I. At the time it seemed such a tangled mess of feeling that I couldn't sort out, still couldn't sort out all these years later. But learning about her, who she is now, what she's been through, what she's overcome and what she's been capable of, I see what went wrong. I didn't have the same capacity to give that she had."

I remembered Sister Anne's words. *Her heart was broken. She told me she had nothing left to give, but she gave the children so much. She gave all of herself.*

And then it was Vera's words I was repeating, the voice that had spoken to me on the Nite Hawk show a short while before. "Love is something that has to be earned." I added: "I didn't earn it. Not with her. Not with you."

Some time passed before Connie said, "I guess it's true then."

"What is?"

A commotion had broken out near the door. Loud laughter and shouting from the Bridge-and-Tunnel table. Another diner shouting for them to shut the hell up. A plate fell, cracked apart on the hard floor. Alphonse was hurrying toward the table to settle things down.

"What's true?" I leaned toward Connie to hear over the ruckus.

"Great minds *do* think alike." She fingered the rim of her coffee cup, looked at me with a tenderness that hurt. "I reached the same conclusion. I've been waiting for the right time to tell you. That I can't go on this way. That it has to be more or—" Her eyes, though moist again, kept the tears in check. "You need someone else. Maybe it's Vera, I don't know. But it's not me. And I—I need someone else too. I used to think *some*thing was better than nothing, that this half-love we shared was better than being alone. But maybe it's not. Maybe it takes being alone to scare you into finding what makes you whole."

It took me a few moments to say, "Yes." It didn't seem enough, that one small word, but I wasn't sure what to add. The noise in the diner had reached a wild-party level which made the silence between us feel even deeper.

She pulled off her wig, stuffed it into her purse. Her eyes dry now, oddly serene. She smoothed her hair, said, "I need to stay here a few minutes alone. Get used to it. Without you."

I waited what seemed like a long time before touching her hand. What I expected to feel was a coldness, a chill, but it was the same warm hand I'd touched so many times before. I stood up, walked unsteadily toward the door.

It wasn't until I was on the street that I thought I should have thanked her, for all those times she was there for me, helping me through a bad night. I considered going back in to tell her but seeing her through the window, her eyes fixed on the seat I'd vacated, it seemed wrong to disturb her solitude.

I promised myself I'd write it down in a letter to her.

PART TWO

South Carolina, Late June 1995

57

Twelve hours in a rented Chevy.

The long southward tilt of I-95.

My eyes flicking between the road and the rearview mirror.

My mind fielding questions. The kind without answers.

Who was this woman I was hoping to find? I thought I knew. I thought I'd understood—from her journals, from what Sister Anne said, from what her husband said—the woman she'd become over the years. A woman capable of so much love and, yet, if Sue's assessment was accurate that she didn't want to be found, why hadn't she opted for the means of escape society provides? A formal separation, a divorce. What was she running from? Or to? And why in this way? Secretly, without explanation.

To simply run off, that seemed a cowardly way to handle the situation—especially for a woman who appeared anything but cowardly in terms of what she'd endured. Maybe *cowardly* was the wrong word. It seemed *ignoble*. For a woman of such grace and compassion.

Who are you to judge? the inner voice asked.

I'm trying to understand.

And what do you know about nobility? You had an affair with her, a married woman. And she, with you. An affair. What some might call a cheap affair.

It was love: unwavering, from the heart.

There you go again, justifying your failures, your sins.

Love supersedes morality.

So you say.

Love justifies itself.

So you'd like to believe.

The road stretched ahead, the flow of traffic fast-moving

and endless. The miles, like thoughts, rolled on and on.

And what about Sue? What was she setting me up for this time? Was I once again acting against my better judgment?

Possibly, yes.

Probably, yes.

But what were my options? Her words repeated themselves in my addled brain: *You don't have a choice. Not if you want to see Vera again.*

The miles, the questions.

The rearview mirror my constant guardian. Who pulled in after me when I stopped for gas or food? Who pulled out after me when I got back on the road?

Knowing—you can't have one without the other—the hunter was also the hunted.

Finally reaching the Carolina coast. The day's light beginning to fade. The Hidden Nook cabins set back off the road, down a narrow driveway cut between tall pines.

In the parking lot I killed the engine, sat there with my hands gripping the wheel. Too much coffee had left me both wide awake and exhausted. On edge, fearful.

The previous night—a lifetime ago, it seemed—had been short, sleepless. I'd packed some essentials and wrote a check for the next month's mortgage payment. How easy it was, I thought, and the realization sobered me, for a single man like myself to leave his life behind.

58

In the graying light of dusk, I didn't bother to check in at the office.

.38 in hand, I took a path through the trees to the cabin where Sue said she was staying.

Cabin 6. The Sea Breeze.

Where Vera and I had stayed those years ago, our one night of relative luxury, after several days of sleeping outdoors. The most private of the cabins, set off as it was from the others, across the driveway and beyond a grove of trees.

The cabin appeared at the path's end. From beyond the dunes, the steady shuffling sound of the ocean.

In the shadow of the pines, I waited. If I was being set up again, I wanted to know what I was facing.

Several minutes passed. Sue appeared in the living room window. No one else visible.

I moved to the steps that led to the rear door.

The handle wouldn't turn.

Through the window I could see the kitchen which opened into the living area, a counter with three stools the only separation between the rooms. A part, not all, of the living room was visible. Into that partial view Sue came, pacing. She stopped to light a cigarette then turned, her back to me, to face the wide front window that looked out on the dunes and the beach and the ruffled white of the ocean waves.

I held the .38 at my side.

When I rapped on the glass she turned, startled, and made her way squinting through the kitchen's murky light. "You're here," she said as if surprised, when she pulled the door back.

"Did you think I wouldn't come?"

"I don't know, I—" She saw the gun in my hand and bolted the door behind me. "You had every reason not to trust me—" In the living room she turned on a lamp. "Did they hurt you bad?"

"Bad enough."

"I'm so sorry for that. I'm trying to make amends."

She reached to touch the bruise on my forehead but I pushed her hand away. "I can still walk and talk."

Except for its wood and rattan furnishings, the room was empty. The bedroom door stood open, darkness inside. I looked in. No one was there.

"Where is she?"

"She's not here." Turning away, she jabbed her cigarette into an ashtray on the coffee table. When she looked at me there was, amid a cold defiant determination, a hint of apology in her eyes. "She left. This morning."

"To go where?"

"An island. Off the coast."

It took me a moment to recall the name. "Shepherd's Island."

"You know it?"

"Only that she mentioned it a few times. After our trip down here, years back. She'd read about it. Said we should go some time. We never did."

"Another regret?"

"One of many." I studied her warily, this woman so meticulously put together in her cashmere sweater and short skirt, her slim legs, her hair pulled back to reveal her clear dark eyes, her broad determined face. "So this was another one of your lies."

"It wasn't a lie. She left—unexpectedly."

"To avoid me?"

"To give herself more time."

"For what?"

"To prepare herself. She's anxious about seeing you—after all this time." She lit another cigarette and stood back, studying me. "Surely you can understand that, can't you?"

"I'm not sure what I understand anymore."

She gave me a half smile. “You can put the gun away.”

“I’ll keep it handy.”

“I know you’re upset with me—”

“You’re a master at understatement.”

“*Furious*, then.”

“You’re getting warmer.”

“I don’t blame you, but no one’s going to hurt you here.” She smiled again, though it did little to reassure me.

“What’s she doing there? On the island.”

“She’s in the process of disappearing for good,” Sue said. “We both are.”

59

They'd been talking about it for almost a year, Sue said. A joke at first, a fantasy they'd take turns embellishing. What would it be like to begin life anew? Where would they go? What would they do? Gradually it moved from fantasy to fact. A plan, a goal, a dream they would make come true. Neither of us, Sue said, thought we had any reason to stay behind, and every reason to move on.

She looked at me then in the gray light of the room, said, "You must be famished. You want to talk about this over dinner?"

"I didn't come for the cuisine."

"Of course not. I just thought—" She seemed at a loss for words, before collecting herself, finding her balance again in the role of hostess. "Please sit down. I'll make us a drink. I know I, for one, need something."

She went to a cabinet above the sink and returned with an unopened bottle of Irish whiskey and two glasses. "Please. Sit down." And this time I did, at one end of the rattan couch, pistol in hand, the broad window to the sea behind me, the sound of the ocean muted here inside the cabin.

She was having trouble opening the bottle so I took it from her, undid the plastic wrapping and poured us each a drink. She sat on the opposite end of the couch and crossed her legs, a gesture slow and deliberate enough to draw my attention. Nodding at the bottle she said, "Your favorite, isn't it? Irish whiskey?"

"I'm surprised you remembered."

"I remember more than you think." She tugged at the hem of her skirt which rode well above her knees, another gesture careful enough to draw attention to itself.

She raised her glass. "To the vanishing past."

60

It was Vera, Sue said, who pushed them to go through with it. After Devon's death, she saw no point in going on with Norm. She'd never felt like a particularly good wife to him. She felt guilty because she couldn't love him the way she knew she was capable of loving a man. She was always holding something back.

"And there was another thing," Sue said, lighting a cigarette, drawing on it quickly and heavily.

"The Blue Flower."

She nodded yes. "She was afraid. She was sure in a weak moment she would succumb." She drew on her cigarette, let the smoke drift toward the darkening window. "Which is where I come into the picture." She finished her drink and poured herself another before filling my glass, as well. "I got her involved in something. Something dangerous."

The story she told might have come from the pages of cheap crime fiction. How, in the years after college, she felt aimless and insecure, falling eventually into what she described as a "nasty" drug habit, a habit a dirty cop helped her sustain when she'd lost her job and run out of money to pay for the stuff on her own.

"Monahan," I said.

"Yes." In return, she said, she "helped him out on occasion" in a moonlighting operation he ran out of a housing project on the lower east side.

"The Madison Houses."

"See," she said, amused at something, "you've got it all figured out."

"Not all of it."

"He supplied; some gang there distributed."

"Before he got involved with the Blue Flower," she said

continuing her story, "he would set up local dealers, then relieve them of both their cash and the drugs they were peddling."

Small-time stuff, but lucrative. Her role was in the re-selling of said drugs which sometimes involved clandestine meetings in abandoned parking garages or midtown offices. On one such occasion she'd been forced to kill a client—in self–defense as it turned out, but all the video showed (unbeknownst to her, he had one of his men tape the transaction) was her firing at an apparently unarmed man. The killing had gained some notoriety at the time, was still a cold case in police files.

"Once he became Blue Flower's main supplier, he wanted to use me in another capacity, on much more than an occasional basis. He wanted to expand, sell the stuff to high-end dealers in Westchester and Connecticut. He saw me as his chief emissary. No more local crews for this part of his enterprise.

"That's when I knew I had to get out. Vera's insistence, you might say, came along at the right time."

"He was the sponsor of that little party in the park?"

"He knows everything I do, everyone I talk to. He knows everything that goes on in the Madison Houses, too. That junkie you talked to, Marcos, works for the crew that works with him. *Did work*," she corrected herself. "Lookout or messenger, sometimes both." She leaned forward, stubbed out her cigarette. "I've been clean now for almost seven years, but when he asks for a 'favor,' I have to do it. Whenever I start to resist, he forces me to watch that tape. The lock and chain on my freedom. You know what it's like to feel that helpless?"

She poured herself another drink. "Believe me, the last thing I wanted to do was set you up. And believe me twice, that was the last *favor* I'll ever do for the man." She raised her glass in a mock farewell, the repentance in her eyes filtered through a new found sense of liberation.

"The picture of you and Vera in that bar in the Alphabet—"

"My tragic flaw." She took a long, deep breath and exhaled slowly. "I wasn't a true friend to her."

"Meaning what?"

"Meaning I never got over my jealousy. Because she had so much love in her life. First Norm, then you, then Devon. Her capacity to feel in such a selfless way."

Like a guilty child, she looked at me, holding her glass in her trembling hand. "So one misguided night, when she was feeling particularly low, I brought her into my shadow world. I re-introduced her to Monahan who, ever since those times we double-dated, had this thing for her he couldn't get over. He'd been after me to bring her around but it wasn't for him that I did it. I had my own devious reasons. And sure enough he was quick to offer her the gift of the Blue Flower, or anything else she wanted. You see, he wanted her anyway he could get her. And he was looking for another *emissary*, for what he saw as his expanding market. He put the stuff in her hand—we were in that awful dive—told her she could use the ladies room, that's what it was there for: '*Go ahead, hon, compliments of the house, see how high the universe truly is.*'"

She looked at me directly, held my gaze. "I did it as a test, to see if she would fall as far I had." She drank deeply, finishing off what was left in her glass. "She came close. She was actually on her way to the ladies room that night when I intercepted her. I told her I had a better idea. Something that would work for both of us. And I pulled her out of there.

"You see," Sue said to me, pouring herself another drink. "There was one thing that had been standing in our way, preventing us from following through on our plans for escape. *Money*. What would we live on if we disappeared? Neither of us had the means for that. But that night, by way of the vagaries of serendipity, I'd found the answer.

"It was too perfect," she said, "the way all the pieces fit. As I said, Monahan wanted Vera to work for him as my partner—two classy looking broads to give his new enterprise a white glove—or should I say white lace—glamour. He wanted her anyway he could get her—if not by hooking her on Blue Flower then by making her part of his expanding criminal empire. For Vera and me, it was our ticket to freedom.

"One shot, one deal, one night. We'd be in and out, then gone for good. Vera was hesitant at first but it didn't take much to convince her; you see, that old Vera, the risk-taker, never completely died. She knew it was our only way out. So we left Manhattan in a rented car with a trunk load of heroin buried in Costco shopping bags. Made the drop at a rest stop off the Merritt near New Canaan. We didn't drive back into the city with the cash like we were supposed to. Of course we had to give the slip to the carful of crew members he had behind us as back-up, but that wasn't all that hard."

I was dumbfounded. "You stole Monahan's money?"

"We thought of it as *our* money by then. After all, we were taking the brunt of the risk, weren't we? It would have been *our* asses in jail if we'd gotten caught, not his."

"There are easier ways to commit suicide."

"We didn't think of it that way. Lucky for us." She sat back and smiled, proud of herself. "And here we are."

61

What do you say to a story like that?

She poured herself another drink. From far off came the muffled rush of surf. "You were a big help to us, you know," she said with a short laugh, "on how to disappear. We followed the steps one of your characters used in your last novel. We stopped using credit cards, closed out bank accounts, called each other on pay phones, anything to hide the fact that we existed. And—"

"—you set up false trails. At least Vera did. Portland and St. Paul. It was something I considered when I first began looking for her but I got distracted, lost the thread of it with everything that followed."

"Of course," Sue said, "there was one more complication. No end to complications, is there?" She laughed at that. "In the days leading up to our big night, Vera was afraid Norm might suspect something was up, that she wouldn't be able to hide her anxiety, her—preparations for leaving. In fact he'd been suggesting they take a spur-of-the-moment vacation now that school was out, get away to relax for a few days, that sort of thing. So she made a rash decision. She up and left for Mercycrest one night, taking nothing with her but a change of clothes stuffed into her camera bag. And that would have been okay except that Monahan found out she'd disappeared. I hadn't counted on you making that visit to his apartment. So I had to calm him down, assure him she just needed a few days to herself, that she'd be back on time to complete our business transaction, that he hadn't a single thing to worry about."

Sue's smirk said it all. Deception was clearly a game where she considered herself the victor. "Everything else went according to plan. We switched cars, zig-zagged our way down here. One night outside Baltimore. One night outside Richmond. In case we were being tailed. And then, of course, another precaution. Hiding out here before heading off to our final destinations."

She looked to me with a schoolgirl's innocence. "So how did we do? Do we get an *A*?" The repentance, the guilt, was long gone from her eyes. In its place and in her smile there was undisguised flirtation.

It seemed beside the point now but I was still angry with her—dumbstruck as well, at her tale—and I wanted to wipe away at least some of her smugness. "It's not that easy, you know, to disappear under the best of circumstances—and this situation, to say the least, is far from the best. And I'm not only talking about the physical part. There's the emotional component, too. It's leaving behind everything and everyone you know. Friends, acquaintances, the city itself, all the world you knew. You'll be saying goodbye to all of it."

Her smile was gone. The flirtatiousness, too. She watched me with her hard, steady eyes. "Haven't you ever thought about beginning your life over again? The possibilities? Getting rid of everything you don't want, all that hellish baggage. Starting fresh. Doesn't that have any appeal to you?"

I sipped the whiskey, glancing at the dark sky above the ocean. "I guess it does. Or else I wouldn't be here now."

Sue nodded her agreement. It seemed, for that moment at least, that we understood one another. "One of the things I can't forgive you for," I said. "The way you manipulated me. You led me on with a few tidbits of information, and withheld the rest."

"Such a harsh word, *manipulate*."

"What would you call it?"

"My allegiance was torn between trying to protect what Vera and I were planning, and what I thought I owed you for your tenacity, your devotion to the cause. What finally decided things was that I knew, at heart, she wanted to re-connect with you."

We sat in silence, nursing our drinks, night settling beyond the window. The rush of the ocean seemed louder now. Silver-rimmed waves flicking at the darkness.

Finally Sue set down her glass and rose, sighing, her

words charged with a gentle sense of finality. "You have two choices for sleeping," she said.

I drained my glass, set it down beside hers and tapped the couch. "This will be fine."

"Your loss," she said, her shoulders stiffening, her smile tight. She turned away, walking with the slightest suggestion of sway in her hips.

Enough to make her point.

I asked, "Out of curiosity, why aren't you on the island now, with her?"

"Maybe I wanted some alone time with you. To clear the air. To—" A smile, a hint of one, uncoiling. "—whatever."

"That's it?"

She gave me a look that said I should know better. "You heard my story. I guess I got to a point I couldn't live with my deceit anymore."

"So Vera doesn't know you manipulated her, too?"

"There's that word again. I prefer to think that, in the end, I helped her get what she wanted. I hope she'll never find out my less savory intentions." She gave me a pointed look.

That was a promise I wouldn't make. If she was expecting one, she must have let it go, because the tightness in her face eased.

"More to the point," she said, "is that we really want different things. Vera is determined to do this island thing—this connection to her younger self, to the children there. She wants a quiet life, a place to do her photography, a place to find some peace."

"And you?"

"I want excitement, bright lights, city life. I want Paris."

When the bedroom door closed behind her, I poured another drink. My last, I promised myself. Something to help me sleep.

I was standing by the window, looking across the dunes at the beach and the silver-spitting tongues of the waves when the bedroom door opened behind me. Sue stood there in a white robe, her face expressionless, her eyes watching me. Slowly she untied the belt, the robe parting to reveal a partial view of her breasts, her flat tanned stomach, her long sleek legs.

She held that position a moment before slowly closing the door.

62

In the morning, she was gone.

She'd left nothing behind but the whiskey. Not even coffee which I badly needed.

Under a heavy sky I walked on the beach, away from the cabins.

An occasional bungalow was set back on the dunes but the beach itself was empty, white and pristine, without evidence of human interference. The wind grew stronger, cooler. Changing direction it seemed, coming off the water, tearing at my eyes, drawing away my breath. Another fifteen minutes of walking until the fuzziness in my head began to clear.

On the horizon the sky had taken on a charcoal color. A swirl of rain clouds thickening and slowly moving landward. The surf rushing in, gray and snarling.

From the living room, watching the storm advance beyond the wide glass window, I called Norm Davison. I owed him at least that much.

Told him where I was.

Told him I'd located Vera.

"I know," he said.

I was taken aback. "How? How do you know?"

There was a bitterness in his voice stronger than anything I'd heard from him before. "I had you followed. That's how."

63

The rain came at nightfall.

Gusting across the lawn of the Hidden Nook Cabins. Hammering the tin roof of the office.

The night clerk jerked awake at the sound of my insistent knocking. He'd dozed off reading *How to be an Awesome Private Eye*, the book flat and open on the desk, having served as a pillow.

His name was Clayton Poole. It was his habit to lock the door after midnight; he didn't like to be taken by surprise. He'd confided this to me later in one of our talks.

Through the window I watched him close his book, tuck it under his arm like a good luck charm and make his way with a groggy, uneven step across the room. When he opened the door, he found me standing there, rain pelting my denim jacket, hair whipped in a frenzy by the wind.

"Coffee," I said. "The machine in my room isn't working."

He looked as though he didn't believe me, but he took a container and went to the pot warming on the table. "You picked a helluva night to begin your vacation," he said.

The reason I'd given earlier in the day when I'd checked in.

"Yes, yes. Helluva night." I'd brought the dampness into the room with me. The wet smell of rain mixed with the aroma of coffee.

"Will you be staying with us long?" he asked.

When I checked in I'd revealed little, if anything, other than to say I was taking over Cabin 6 from my friend, who had had to leave unexpectedly. I'd scrawled a phony name and address onto the registration card, and paid in cash.

"Not that long," I said. "It all depends."

He looked at me as if to say, *on what*?

"We'll have to see," I said, "how things go."

He nodded as if he understood. "Shouldn't be a problem. We're not heavily booked this week."

When he handed me the container, cap snugly in place, I asked, "Any word on when this is going to let up?"

"By morning, they say."

We listened to the rain thundering across the roof. The wind a whistling scream of sound where it struck the windows.

"Depends on the wind, though. If it shifts, as they predict, it'll drive the storm out to sea. If not, the front could stall out here for most of tomorrow."

I thanked him for the coffee. At the door, I said, "One more thing. You expecting anybody else this evening?"

"No reservations, no."

He waited a moment before adding: "In this business, though, you never can tell. Anybody can show up out of nowhere."

64

The rain had turned the driveway into a river of mud. I slipped, half slid my way across it, bully-shoved by the tail wind coming off the ocean. Inside the Chevy I set the coffee on the dash, smoothed back my wet hair then wriggled out of my jacket.

My vigil had begun shortly after dark and I'd been sitting more or less in the same position, slouched in the front seat, ever since. Without a doubt I'd been expecting Monahan or one or more of his cronies; but after my call to Davison it seemed a pretty good bet *he* might be on his way, as well.

Backed into the trees like this, I had a fully protected view of the driveway. To the right I could see the short distance to the two-lane highway that brought me here; to the left I could see the Ocean View cabins, all five of them in a line adjacent to the motel office, and beyond that a section of beach with the ocean raging against it. Directly ahead, through a thin line of trees, a section of dunes was visible, the Sea Breeze cabin tucked in behind them. I'd become, I hoped, an unobserved eye in the darkness, which gave me at least the illusion of safety. Though I kept hearing Davison's voice, rife with bitterness, saying *I had you followed.* Was I being watched even now? Was the Hidden Nook property, in a way I hadn't yet detected, under surveillance?

I had the .38—under the cover of a magazine—on the seat beside me.

And if Monahan or Davison did show up, what then?

I'd been pondering that, with no resolution, for most of the day and through the long hours of dusk. The sky growing more ominous over the ocean. The day's last light taking on a strangely luminous, eerie green light: the color, I thought, that would accompany the world's end, the final startling burst of light before eternal darkness.

I sipped the coffee and tried to shake off such apocalyptic thoughts. My world wasn't ending, not yet anyway. It was truer to say that it was in transition and, for a moment, doubts assailed me.

Had I taken on more than I could handle?

Maybe. *Probably.*

Yet this was equally true: something necessary had been missing in my life. And given the opportunity, the chance for love, wouldn't any man grab that chance?

The truth.

It set things straight, intolerant as it was of self-pity or doubt. It was what I had now instead of God.

And this also was true: the reason I didn't go straight to the island to find Vera. Whatever trouble might lie ahead, I wanted to keep it *away* from her. I would settle the score here with whoever showed up.

65

The pin-prick lights of a car's head beams flashed momentarily on the highway, before the lights swung around, illuminating the driveway.

I stiffened, leaning forward for a better look. The vehicle in question a maroon minivan, not Davison's Dodge Dart or Monahan's black Caddy.

The van stopped in the turnaround alongside the motel office. Motor running, lights on. A few seconds passed before the door opened. A squat, balding man hurried through the rain to the office door, trying the knob first, then pounding insistently with the flat of his hand.

It took the clerk a full minute or more to open the door. The heavy-set man disappeared inside, but then re-emerged surprisingly quickly. Without bothering to move the van, he opened the passenger side doors to release its occupants: a woman about his size, and two equally oversize pre-teens, a boy and a girl. They followed him in line—each with the same droop-shouldered walk—to the first of the cabins where he unlocked the door and stood aside as they traipsed inside, one after the other. Then he returned to the van and removed two over-sized suitcases. The weight of them, one in each hand, contributed to his shrunken look as he trudged back to the cabin.

Through my windshield's running-water blur, the cabins looked dingy and sorrowful: a dull gray settlement huddled below the black sky. All five of the small dwellings were identical: pitched roof wooden boxes, each with a narrow front porch, each in a varying state of decay. All were dark save for that first cabin where yellow light now burst through the side window.

The only other light came from the windows of the motel office and the red neon VACANCY sign attached to its roof.

I shifted on the seat, stretched my legs in the space beneath the dash. The rain gusting off the ocean slashed across the cabin roofs, came hissing over the Chevy's metal. Pine boughs thrashed in the wind, their joints creaking. Hot as hell in the car but the rain beat too hard to open the windows even a crack.

On the highway, car lights came slowly toward the turnoff. Again I tensed, squinting through the windshield's blur.

The car picked up speed, drove past the motel entrance, then was lost to view beyond a dense cluster of trees.

I reached for the coffee, held it to my lips before sipping. It was already cold.

The dashboard clock read ten past two.

I stared at the vacancy sign that bled sour light into the darkness and listened to the thrash of pine boughs, the hiss of rain. My entire life, it seemed, had been spent this way.

Watching.

Waiting.

Observing, from a distance, the lives of others.

66

The second of the late night guests arrived shortly before 2:30.

The car, a black one, came in slowly off the highway. The rear license plate flashed by too quickly to read.

The car—I could see now it was a large, late-model Mercedes—pulled in behind the van outside the motel office. The figure that emerged—a tall, angular man dressed in a dark jacket, dark pants—stood still a moment, hand braced against the Mercedes' door, surveying the scene before him. He straightened up then and walked unhurried with a stiff, military bearing through the stain of red light to the office door.

When he re-appeared minutes later he walked in the same stiff unhurried way, taut-shouldered against the dampness. He backed his car away from the van and drove across the muddy grass to a makeshift driveway between cabins 2 and 3. Stepping out, he carried a small, duffel-type overnight bag. Before his tall shadow slipped inside the cabin, the Mercedes' lights flashed once; the car horn emitted a single beep.

I strained to see through the wet windshield. The rain had let up, replaced by mist through which shadows moved in pale, shifting light.

Several moments passed before the cabin door opened and the shadow stood on the narrow porch. A match flamed. The glow of the man's cigarette moving in a downward arc from his lips, the exhaled smoke barely distinguishable from the mist.

I set the wipers in motion. The rain beginning again, not quite as hard. Each sweep of the blades bringing a staggered image. The cigarette's arc from hand to mouth. The thin shadow-man turning to face the sea. The glowing point of the cigarette spinning outward toward the beach and vanishing.

Wind-driven rain rumpling in sheets across the sand.

Then the shadow was gone from the porch.

The cabin's rear window awakened briefly with light before going dark once more.

The rain suddenly tapered off again. I donned my jacket, collar turned up, and walked toward the cabins until I was close enough to read the Mercedes' plates: *New Jersey*.

That he was from the New York area raised the possibility of a connection to Monahan or Davison. A possibility I didn't relish contemplating.

More than likely it was simply coincidence, I told myself. There had to be a lot of travelers from the tri-state area down here, didn't there?

In the office, behind the counter, the night clerk was hunkered over his book. "More coffee?" he asked.

"No, no. I'm good. Having trouble sleeping is all. Damn rain's so loud."

"It's that darn tin roof on the Sea Breeze. I keep tellin' the boss we got to replace it."

"Yeah, guess that's what it is." I loosened my coat collar, ran a hand through my damp hair. "Say, I couldn't help but notice that car that just came in. The one with New Jersey plates. You always get so many of us Yankees down here?"

"It's the ocean, you know. Folks can't stay away. And we're close to Hilton Head. Folks who don't want to spend money on a luxury condo, well, we're a cheaper alternative."

"Oh, I see. Thought maybe he was a regular. Came here often."

"Nope. Never been here before, far as I know. I been here six years." He beamed at me, proud of that fact. "Night shift gives me plenty of time to study up." He held the book up so I could read the title. "I'm aiming to be a shamus someday." He smiled self-consciously. "A private investigator," he added.

"I'm familiar with the term."

"I'm really set on it. I practice all the time. With people, I mean. Try to figure them out, size them up."

"Bet you're good at it."

His eyes fired up at the compliment. "I'm getting better. Night clerk here's a perfect job for it. Studying folks, I mean."

"You know, that's funny. I do the same thing. Studying people like you do. Figuring out what makes them tick."

"Really? You a P.I?"

"I'm the curious type, that's all." I leaned against the counter, buddy to buddy. "Like that guy just came in, for instance. Middle of the night, by his lonesome. What do you figure his deal is?"

The clerk nodded, pursed his lips, taking the question seriously. "He did raise some flags, didn't he? Man with a purpose, I'd say. Something heavy. No time for chit-chat. Not real sociable, you know? On his way somewhere fast."

"He didn't say *where* he was going, how long he'd be here?"

"Nope. Didn't say anything, really. 'Cept he needed a room. For a few nights."

"A *few* nights?"

"Paid in advance."

"His name wasn't Wilson, was it?" A cheesy ploy, hoping the kid might fall for it, give me a name in return. "Reminds me a lot of a guy I knew in the army. From what I could see of him. Al Wilson. That was my buddy's name. From Jersey City."

"That's not the name he gave," the clerk said. "He paid in cash. Like you. Boss tells me not to push for an address, if the customer pays in cash. People got a right to their privacy, he always says. For a little while longer, at least. Till the Fed and the corporations take it all away."

"I'm with him on that."

"So what do you think? About my profile. The guy in black."

"I think you're right. Someone with a purpose. Someone with a job to do. Tailing somebody maybe."

The clerk's face lit up again with pleasure. "Sometimes I make up these scenarios, you know? About the guests who come here. I imagine these situations—crime scenes I guess you'd call them. What if this happened, or that? How would I react? How would I solve the crime?"

"Sounds like good practice."

"You think so?"

"Definitely. Maybe we can compare notes again tomorrow. See what we can figure out about this guy."

"I'd like that. I'd really like that."

"Could be the dangerous type, you know? Could even be packing."

The clerk's eyes widened. "A hit man, you mean?"

"Could be. Let's keep tabs on him. Check in with each other as soon as we know something."

"Double-team him, right? Two sets of eyes are better than one."

"That's the idea."

The clerk thrust out his hand. "A pleasure to meet you, Mr.—?" He hesitated. "It was hard to read your name on the registration card."

"Walker," I said, for once in my life thankful for the anonymity, that he hadn't read my books, hadn't seen my photo plastered on the book jackets. "And the pleasure's mine," I added, shaking his hand.

"Hey, it's almost three." He flicked on the radio perched on the desk behind him. "Right now the Nite Hawk's coming on. From your neck of the woods. Wanna listen? We get pretty good reception middle of the night like this."

I was moving toward the door. "Gotta get some shut-eye."

"Helps me through the night," the clerk said. "The dude understands the secrets of the human heart."

As the door closed behind me, I heard the familiar voice rise against the falling rain.

What do we do with the night?

67

Through the scratchy haze of static on the car's radio, his voice fading in and out, I listened to the story of a night security guard at an outdoor parking lot on the upper west side of Manhattan. "Feels like I'm in a maze with no way out," he said. "Cars all around me, row after row, chain-link fence the only damn thing keepin' away the thieves. They come at me from all sides, from anywhere—the river, the rail yards, the alleys—lookin' for batteries, side mirrors, head lights, any damn thing they can get their hands on in a jiffy. Every night it's dread and more dread. For chris-sakes, it's a bad dream that don't quit till the sun rises. And whaddaya think they give me to fight the bastards off? A night stick, for chris-sakes. Goddamn, can you believe it? What the hell good's a night stick against a gun? Or two or three guns? What kinda chance I got?"

Then it was my own dream world I'd fallen into.

Where I was fighting hard.

First against the very fatigue that brought me there. The force that prevented me keeping my vigil, that kept my eyes locked tight against the rainy night: the water that ran in rivulets along the driveway, the dark and dismal cabins, the strip of highway that was the artery to what I was guarding myself against.

I tried to wake but couldn't.

Dark-suited figures stalking me. Shadows barely discernible in the mist.

That was the problem, I heard myself telling someone, *the shape of the enemy is never the same, disguising itself as this familiar thing or that, refusing to come forth and identify itself.*

Then I was deep in conversation with Vera, explaining that I was trying to reach her, that one way or another I had been trying to reach her all my life.

Movement outside the car awakened me: to morning, to light.

Water droplets trembling on the windshield, glimmering on leaves. Puddles on the driveway reflecting the sun. On the car's hood, what was left of the rain gathering into tiny beads.

The movement that had brought me back to life occurred at some distance. The family of four emerging from the motel office, each of them with a doughnut in hand. The complimentary Continental breakfast.

7 a.m. on the dashboard clock.

The family heading in tandem for the beach, mom and pop first, son and daughter directly behind, each with a similar waddle-like walk.

When they were out of sight, I moved the Chevy to the designated parking lot before crossing the driveway, heading through the narrow band of trees toward the dunes that formed a fifty foot barrier between the beach and the Sea Breeze cabin. Stiffness in my knees and hips and left shoulder. After-effects of a cramped night. And of the beating in the park.

I was remembering the night I'd spent here with Vera. The panic upon awakening to find she wasn't in bed. Calling out her name to the empty rooms. Dressing quickly and hurrying out.

Behind the cabin, a sandy path disappeared into an area of squat, dense scrub pine, the limbs of which had long been twisted and tortured into grotesque shapes by the sea wind and salt air. The path took the form of a loosely shaped loop that led out to the beach, several hundred feet from the cabin. There I'd found her sitting near the dunes, arms clasped around her knees, a portrait of serenity in contrast to the wild beating of my heart. I'd thought I would surely die if I lost her.

In a sense that had proven to be true. Only it had been a longer, slower death than I'd imagined.

Now I followed the loop path out to the beach, wondering how things were going to play out, what pieces remained of the puzzle.

As always, an incomplete puzzle.

One of my characters once mused that life was such a crooked deal, each man clinging to the sliver of what he knew or *thought* he knew, chasing a closure which—by definition—would never be found.

Far down the beach, beyond the motel office, I had a view of the Ocean View cabins, squat and undisturbed under the bluest of skies, the chrome on the Mercedes—the only car parked there—flashing back sunlight into the windless air.

No sign of the car's owner.

No sight yet of the man in the dark suit from New Jersey.

68

Nostalgia drove me inland, away from the coast. If I couldn't have Vera right now, I could at least re-live a memory of her.

Lowland marshes gave way to small hills, thick forests. Eventually the road flattening out, opening into farm country. Fields of corn and soybeans on one side, peach orchards on the other.

My first gig for a magazine, my first paid article, the first and only overnight road trip Vera and I had taken. At that time the commune was the South's longest surviving psychedelic enclave, inhabited when we arrived by the children of the original founders.

What was left of it now was one main structure: a long double-wide trailer, standing close to the road. Behind it were scattered a half dozen smaller trailers, and beyond the trailers a barn at the edge of a field that sprawled back to the distant tree line.

But for an aging pick-up parked near the barn, no vehicles of any kind were present. The double-wide itself had broken windows, rust stains beneath them and along its roof line. The outlying trailers, especially those closest to the road, appeared to be falling in on themselves, metal siding discolored by time and neglect. Waist-high grass and weeds filled the yard and the field behind it.

On the back wall of the double-wide the once-bright colors of a rainbow mural had faded into the weather-beaten metal. Rising from the grass a wooden sculpture of a man, hand raised in a peace sign, had been badly mutilated: the head and one arm had been cut off, the torso pock-marked front and back with bullet holes.

Several other smaller sculptures, of abstract design and in various stages of decay, lay scattered about the yard.

At the time Vera and I stayed there, two hundred people or more jammed into the yard for nightly celebrations, though I wasn't sure now what they'd been celebrating. The full moon, I think. The open-ended, wildly diverse philosophies of youth. A future with no constraints, no visible boundaries. There had been a lot of heavy drumming interspersed with interludes of silence and the sound of a single flute, mournful and eerie, played by the leader of the commune, a woman called Harmonia.

She was indiscriminately seductive, a creature of ambiguous sexuality. At times coming onto Vera. Other times coming onto me. And still other times trying to ensnare both of us in her web of flirtation. Which led to a running joke between Vera and me: inventing new and ingenious ways to avoid the woman's unflagging pursuit—zealous guardians as we were of our intimacy.

The field that spread out beyond the trailers had been cultivated then, the commune's food supply. Vera and I slept at the edge of it, curled in a sleeping bag. We made love under the moon. No drugs. No third party additions. No enhancements of any kind. Simply ourselves. Flesh to flesh against the flannel lining.

Reverie interrupted.

A man emerging from the barn where the pick-up was parked. An aging hippie. Grey hair pulled back in a ponytail, bandanna around his neck, faded tie-dyed T-shirt, beat-up jeans and sandals.

"Help you?"

I tried to connect him to the members of the commune that I remembered, but he seemed far too grizzled, too *old* for the lively and colorful characters who'd inhabited this place. Ten years takes a toll on all of us, I reminded myself. But still I could find no place for him in my memory bank.

His face had long been abused by the sun: lines, crevices, spotted skin. He squinted with dull, glazed eyes. Something off about him. Too much Speed or pot, too much LSD. Or maybe I'd simply caught the old guy napping.

"What happened?" I asked.

"You *see* what happened." The old man spit the words. He shifted his weight; he held a hackey sack in his hand, squeezing it thoughtlessly. "Used to be tents all around that field there, corn and beans and tomatoes growin' in the middle. Music everywhere. Good vibes."

His lips moved before the next words came. His eyes growing intense. "You should have seen it."

Out of curiosity I asked him if he knew what happened to the woman who ran things here.

"Harmonia?"

"Yes."

He looked surprised at the question. "She's still here."

"Where?"

"In that field, in them trees, in what's left of them trailers."

"Dead?" I asked.

"Eternal," he said.

He turned to go, a trifle unsteadily, back toward the barn.

"Haven't seen a hackey sack in quite some time," I called after him.

The man stopped and held out his hand, lifting the blue and gold sack up to the light, as though it were a jewel that showed itself to best advantage in the sun. "Better days," he said.

69

At the Hidden Nook, I was relieved to see the black Mercedes gone. Just a coincidence, after all, that he'd shown up last night, that he was from "my neck of the woods," as the night clerk would say. Just a fear conjured up by my over-heated imagination.

One less thing to worry about.

I walked down the beach to a point where the coastline formed a rocky promontory. From there I looked eastward. Shepherd's Island was beyond view, lost in the late afternoon haze, the horizon a dull grey line smeared at the edges.

I stood fast against the rising wind.

For now, this was as close as I would get to Vera.

I felt restless, impatient, impulsive. Wait it out, I told myself. Stick with the plan. Keep her away from whatever trouble's coming.

Through the window of the office, I could see that it was Clayton Poole on duty.

"Day clerk's out sick," he informed me when I stepped inside. "I'm on for a double shift today and tonight." He'd combed his hair in a slicked-back fashion, wet and dark with hair oil. He also wore a pair of rimless glasses. I wondered if he'd decided this improved his image as an aspiring private eye.

I said, "I see our man is gone."

"Oh, no. Just out somewhere. He was in before to pay for another night." He seemed eager to tell me more. "I like your theory about him being a hit man. That got me thinking. He asked me where the town was so he could get to a phone. I told him he could use the office phone right here, but he said that was okay he had to go into town for some supplies anyway. I figure that was just an excuse, that the nature of his call was so private he didn't want anyone to hear. Suspicious, right?"

"Could be."

"So when he left, I snuck into his room to look around. It's at least twenty minutes round trip into town, so I figured I had time. Worst case, if he caught me, I could say I was checking for a leak, or whatever. Guess what I found?"

"I don't know. What?"

"Two M1911's hidden in his duffel bag. Fully loaded."

"Interesting." I knew the gun. A firearm used by the U.S. Military for more than seventy years.

The clerk was wide-eyed at his discovery. "It all adds up, don't it?"

"What does?"

"Your hit man theory. I mean, his having military-grade weapons and all. It ties in with the way he walks, kind of stiff and military-like. And the way he talks. Tight-lipped. Like he's afraid of giving out too much information. I figure maybe he's a mercenary, a gun for hire. What do you think?"

"Did you find anything else? In the room?"

"Nothing that might identify him. Or where he was from. Or where he was going. Which is suspicious, too, right? I mean, like he's totally anonymous. He could be anybody, or nobody."

I patted his shoulder. "Good work, Clayton. You'll be a helluva detective someday."

The kid smiled unabashedly.

"Keep me posted if you learn anything else."

"Will do, Mr. Walker. I sure will do."

"I'll do the same."

"What a team," he said with a beaming smile.

I was on my way back to the beach when the Mercedes turned into the driveway, cruised slowly past me, and parked in its familiar place outside the second cabin.

70

Hugging the uneven edge of the dunes, a man was coming toward me, trudging heavily through the sand.

Other than the approaching figure, I was alone on the beach, the family of four nowhere in sight. I pulled myself into a sitting position, fingered the .38 in my jacket pocket.

The figure was some fifty yards away.

Monahan.

The walk, the trench coat gave him away. He plodded steadily toward me, left arm lost in his coat, right arm hanging close against his leg.

I got slowly to my feet.

Monahan had a mouth full of gum, chewing hard on it as he drew close. "Where you keeping her?"

"You think I'd tell you?"

"We're going to have to have a little talk, you and me."

"So let's talk."

"Not here. Your cabin."

I had no desire to leave the relative safety of the beach, the motel office not far off. "I'd rather talk here."

"I wasn't *asking* you," Monahan said. The trench coat flapped back in the wind, revealing a gun in the man's hand. A Glock 9.

"What, Mike, you gonna shoot me here?"

"If I have to."

The man was bluffing, I felt sure. He needed me. Unless he figured he could track Vera—and of course Sue, too—down on his own. Which, the more I thought about it, was a possibility, given that with all his years on the Force, he would have come into contact with some of the best Skip Tracers around. If Sue or Vera had been at all careless in their journey to erase themselves from society's view. . . if either of them had slipped up even once . . .

Taking in the man's unforgiving hawk-eyed look, I decided not to chance it.

"If you insist."

Monahan chewed his gum harder, waggled the gun at me, at the same time keeping it close to his body. "I insist."

I started on the path, a few feet ahead of Monahan, feeling like a kid being taken down an alley to have the crap beaten out of him.

I have a weapon now, I reminded myself as we plodded through the heavy sand, passing by the twisted arms of the pines. *I have a weapon and I'm not afraid to use it.*

It was a thought I held onto until the path turned one last time and the cabin appeared not more than fifty feet ahead, wood and glass rising from the sand, the back stairs marred by a tall black shadow moving toward us: the man from New Jersey with his arm raised in our direction.

In his hand, a long-barreled handgun as black as the suit he was wearing.

71

This I learned later:

Clayton Poole remained faithful to his surveillance duties all that day.

After the whole affair was over, he gave the local newspaper a full account of his activities—the same account he would give to me in lengthy detail—from the time Monahan arrived.

It began with Clayton crouched at the office window, watching what he was convinced was the latest in a series of unfolding mysterious events: a man in a trench coat walking up the driveway and heading directly to the beach, moving swiftly and with purpose.

The clerk had spent all the hours of his shift, the time he usually spent reading or dozing off, trying to figure things out. Suspicious characters. Shadowy circumstances. Something waiting to happen.

It had all started, he concluded, with the storm. Fiercer than other storms he'd worked through. Nastier. The wind—he'd swear to it—more vicious off the ocean, the surf louder, more relentless, the rain harder and more persistent. An omen—he now saw it for what it was—a sure as hell omen, if there ever was one. Evidenced by the mean and constant hissing of the wind in the pines, geez almighty, an unnerving sound to say the least, boughs raised in fury, clashing against the rain, the sky, geez, the very darkness itself.

A man alone needs comfort in such a storm and he had found that comfort by imagining that an interested, anonymous party had paid him an enormous sum of money to get to the bottom of what was going on. *There's intrigue here, young man, and possibly scandal. Possibly even criminal activity.*

It was the kind of case Clayton had been preparing

himself for. Something to test his sleuthing skills. Oh, there had been situations before this, what he *thought* were cases, involving other guests, other questionable behavior; but the reality had ended up being nothing like what he'd imagined, the behavior in question turning out to be completely innocent, the crimes he'd envisioned nothing more than figments of his over-eager imagination.

But this. This was the real thing. He was sure of it.

First there was the man who called himself Walker, and the two pretty women who had preceded him. Then there was the man's apparent insomnia which didn't go halfway toward explaining why he'd parked his car in that grove of trees off the driveway. Why he'd sat out there in the dark instead of curling up in bed with the heat on and a roof over his head.

Then there was the even more mysterious man in the black suit. Mr. dead-of-the-night-arrival. Mr. mouth-shut-tight-don't-say-a-word. Mr. don't-fill-out-the-registration form-except-for-a-name-so-hastily-scrawled-it-was-impossible-to-read.

There was a connection between the two men, he was sure of that, though what that connection was he couldn't say. Maybe over one of the women. A love triangle. Or maybe Walker and the women were wanted by the police, and the man in black—if he wasn't after all a hit man—was FBI, or some other kind of Fed. Or a P.I. keeping them under surveillance for a jealous third-party.

And then this latest twist in the case: the man in the trench coat who left his car at the end of the driveway. Who didn't bother to check in at the office. Who marched out onto the beach, as if this had all been pre-arranged, as if he knew exactly where he was going, in the direction of the spot where the man who called himself Walker was sitting by the dunes.

Was *he* the jealous lover coming for one of the women? Her husband, maybe? Or possibly a cop on his way to making an arrest? For drugs or arms running? Or maybe something even more sinister? And who was this Walker guy, anyway? Not a straight-shooter, for sure. Holding something back, putting on an overly-friendly act for some as yet undisclosed reason.

Whatever was going to happen was about to happen soon. Any minute. Any moment. Clayton was sure of that. This was the life he'd only been able to dream about, night after night, during the lonely hours of his shift. In his mind, it justified being derelict in his motel clerk duties. If a prospective guest arrived, he would simply have to wait to check in.

He took his camera and locked the office door, hurrying across the driveway, losing his footing on one of the deeper ruts and sending a spray of muddy water over his brand new, spanking-white sneakers and across the hem of his equally white pants, tripping then a second time over a tree root on the short cut he was taking through the grove of pines. His camera flew from his hands and he landed face forward in a bed of pine needles.

As he struggled to his feet, not even bothering to brush the dirt that now extended from the hem to the knees of his white pants, but taking the time to brush the dirt from his jettisoned camera, praying to the Almighty that it would still work, he recited to himself a warning from the surveillance chapter of his textbook: *Jittery nerves can blow your cover*.

Geez, calm yourself the heck down, he told himself.

He glanced around, relieved that the only witnesses to his clumsiness were two sullen-eyed crows in the branches above, and the stolid mute trunks of the pines.

Several deep breaths later, he was proceeding more carefully between the trees in the direction of the dunes and the Sea Breeze cabin, where his hunch told him the crime scene he expected was going to play out.

72

Monahan listed toward the cabin's front door, standing as he had been on the beach, left hand jammed into his trench coat pocket, right hand hanging loose at his side. The only difference was that the hand at his side was empty, the Glock shoved into his shoulder holster, unnecessary at the moment because the man in black—his muscle, who went by the name of CeeCee—stood nearby at the counter that divided the kitchen from the living room. His gun was, for the time being, also out of sight; but mine was not, lying in plain sight on the kitchen counter since it had been confiscated.

I stood in the middle of the room, between them, where I had to shade my eyes against the light flooding through the front window, the one directly behind the couch where the dunes and the beach were visible and the ocean beyond that, awash in the bright morning light.

But it was the side window that drew my attention. My eye had caught some motion there: a bird perhaps, I thought at first, flitting amid the boughs of the pine grove. What I saw now, though, was part of a face, the night clerk's face. Then it was gone.

"So, I'll ask you again," Monahan was saying. He shoved a stick of gum into his mouth, adding to what was already there, and he chomped down on it heavily, calling even more attention to the unflattering fleshiness of his jowls. "Where the hell is Vera?"

"As I've said, she's not here."

Monahan rested his heavy weight against the door, closed his eyes tight as if he might be counting to ten, struggling to contain his temper. "Now tell me something I *don't* know."

How many ways could I tell him the same thing, what he

refused to accept as reality. "As I've said, I was informed Vera was here. That's why I came."

Monahan sneered. "You were *informed*?"

"That's right."

"By who?"

"Let's just say by someone I knew."

"Let's just say you start givin' me some answers or I make your face something you don't recognize."

I threw out a challenge of my own. "Doesn't really matter who told me, does it? What matters is she's not here. What matters is what you're going to do about it."

"Oh, I'll do something about it. You can be damned sure of that." He took a step toward me, swaying with a rage he was losing the battle to control. "You were always a piss-ant faggot, Garrett, you know that? Now you're a piss-ant faggot with a smart mouth."

"I'll take that as a compliment."

The meaty palm of Monahan's hand struck my face full on. I staggered backwards, cringing in anticipation of another blow.

"That's what a smart mouth gets you." He grabbed me by the collar, shoved me back into the arms of CeeCee who held me while Monahan bludgeoned me with his fists. "Where *is* she, asshole?"

I found myself sagging in CeeCee's arms, but I struggled to keep my legs from buckling.

"Where is she?" Monahan began to wheeze, his breathing heavy and rasping, his overweight and out of shape body menacing even as he began to tire. His words were flung out like a mouthful of spit. "*Where—is—she?*"

With bloodied vision, I watched the dimming figure weave before me.

"You don't know where she is, do you?" Monahan was saying. "This is just another one of your fuck-ups. The man who *thinks*, but can't *do*. Who's all words and no action. Who can't get the job done, can't pull the trigger. You're a limp-dick faggot, you know that? Always were, always will be."

I should have kept my mouth shut. I didn't know how much he knew about what *I* knew about his expanding empire; but my better judgment gave way to a viciousness and spite of my own. I couldn't stop myself. "Not so limp I didn't figure out your little Blue Flower gig in the projects. Not so limp I don't know about a few folks who died because of that poison you sell. Not so limp—"

Monahan wouldn't let me finish. "What you don't know is how close you came to your final resting place in the bushes that night in the park. What you don't know is how much you're gonna suffer before I'm through with you."

He came at me again, swinging wildly at my face, chest, arms, belly. The pain seeming to come from everywhere at once.

Finally CeeCee let go of me.

I fell to my knees briefly before pulling myself up and holding on to the counter rim. Inside the pain, the ringing in my ears, words were being spoken.

"Truth is," Monahan was saying, "I don't need you at all. My Skips will find her. Sooner or later. They'll find *both* of them. They've never failed me yet. I was a fool to think you'd be of any use. But I thought, what the hell, maybe the guy *does* know something, maybe he *can* bring me to her. Big mistake. Big son-of-a-bitchin' mistake. I'd of been smarter, I woulda done us both a favor. That way you wouldn't be here now, and I wouldn't have wasted my time chasing your sorry ass. And you, you wouldn't be suffering the way I'm gonna make you suffer."

"You really are insane, aren't you?" I said. "What do you think's going to happen if you do find Vera? She's gonna jump into your arms? You're going to walk off hand in hand?" Despite the pain in my head and in my gut, I pushed away from the counter, standing—albeit unsteadily—on my own. I blinked away the blood in my eyes. "Or is it abduction you have in mind? Kidnapping your game now?"

Monahan drew his shoulders up, his cheeks sucked in as if he might spew not only his gum but all of his bile in my face.

Then he relaxed his shoulders, letting the air drain out of him in a long exhalation of breath. "You see anybody being kidnapped, Cee? We're trying to work this out, is all. Set things straight."

"You can't bully and threaten someone into loving you."

"I know what I want and I go after it, if that's what you mean." He glanced at CeeCee for confirmation. The man, stone-faced, nodded his acknowledgement. "I'm a reasonable man. I'm sure when I talk to her, she'll see things my way. People usually do." He turned a withering look on me. "Even *you*. Once you take a little ride with CeeCee here, I think you'll see things my way, too."

"Or maybe," I added because again I couldn't resist, "you're still counting on getting her hooked first, then having your way."

That seemed to cut to the big man's core. He stiffened. A dull, flat deadness froze the look in his eyes before something blazed there, the light of cruelty re-surfacing full-strength. He reached for his shoulder holster and I thought I was a dead man, then and there. But the former detective caught hold of himself, let his hand drop. His eyes went flat again, dead.

Something moved behind him.

In the corner of the window, the night clerk's face appeared once more. I was the only one who saw him. What the hell did the damn kid think he was doing?

Then the face was gone.

In its place, in the left lower pane, was the boy's hand holding a video camera to the glass.

Monahan moved toward me so that his body blocked much of the window from view. "You're excused."

I stared at him blankly.

"I said, you're excused, numb-nuts." He shoved me toward CeeCee who, in turn, stiff-armed me toward the back door.

At that point I was so dizzy and disoriented I thought I might collapse right there. I caught myself, though, stood still long enough to feel steady again, before CeeCee shoved me one more time toward the door.

Before we reached it, the door swung open, revealing Davison at the threshold.

73

Davison came into the room as if he owned it, nodding at Monahan but keeping his eyes on me.

Hurt and betrayal in his look.

"What the hell you doing here?" Monahan said. "Told you I'd handle it."

Davison ignored him. By accident or design, he was wearing the same brand trench coat as Monahan, both hands shoved deep into his pockets. His shoulders slightly hunched like Monahan's. His face drawn tight in a scowl. He addressed me directly but his question seemed posed for anyone in the room to answer. "Where is she?"

Monahan's laugh was loud and mocking. "He fooled us, man. Joke's on us."

Davison glared at me, the look of hurt and betrayal deepening, as if he couldn't quite make sense of things. "You mean she's not here?"

"That's right," I said.

"I don't understand. You said—"

I shrugged. "I said I'd located her. Apparently she *was* here, then left."

"To go where?"

"We've been through all this, Davison," Monahan cut in. "She's not here. You made the trip for nothing. Deal with it."

Briefly, Davison's air of authority faded. His face had the same tentative, self-conscious look as the night he first knocked on my door. "You've been lying to me from the beginning. You've been holding back what you know." More a lament than an accusation.

I raised my hands, palms-up, in a defensive gesture. "You asked me to do a job. That's what I've been doing."

"Not with any honesty. Not the way I wanted you to."

"You're wasting your time with this jerk-off." Monahan stepped between us, facing Davison, chest out. "Told you I'd handle this."

"Not very well, I'm afraid. You were supposed to tail Garrett. That was your only function. That was the only role I had in mind for you."

"What do you think I've been doing?"

"Acting badly. Acting like a fool." Davison's calm, unruffled manner, the soft-spoken way his words came out, made them seem all the more lethal.

"You're the loser can't keep his wife at home."

"The greatest fool is the one who doesn't know he's a fool," Davison said in the same steely, soft-spoken way.

Monahan raised his shoulders, took a swaggering step closer to him. "I told you we were going to do things *my* way. So back off. And I don't like the way you waltzed your candy-ass in here like you owned the goddamn—"

"You were supposed to tail him, let him lead us to her. It wasn't part of the plan for you to beat him half to death or assassinate him *while* he's tracking her down."

"What do you want from me? The son-of-a-bitch got too—"

"Enough." Davison said with a dismissive wave of his hand. "You failed to execute your assigned duties."

"I'm gonna take care of Garrett. I will—"

"Too late now."

"What are you talking about? What's too late? We don't need this asshole. My skip tracers will find her, just a matter of time and—"

"Then what?" Davison asked matter-of-factly. "You think I'm going to let you take her? How did you just put it? You were going to have a talk with her, make her see things your way? You were going to reach some kind of understanding?"

Sarcasm didn't come naturally to him, but his laugh was genuine in its mockery, dark and venomous. "Did you really think I was going to let a predatory *animal* like you get anywhere near her? When I asked for your help, that was never part of my plan."

"Yours wasn't the only plan," Monahan said.

A face-off. A moment passing.

"I'd like you to leave," Davison said.

A stunned silence.

Monahan glared at him in disbelief, chewing his gum with a sudden, crazed intensity. "Say again?"

"Your services are no longer required."

"No one talks to me that way."

"I'll say it once more if you'd like. I want you to leave the premises. I want you gone." Again it was the controlled, steel-edged steadiness of his voice that was most unnerving.

Monahan stiffened, drew himself to his full height. "You don't have the balls to back that up."

A beat of time.

A bridge of silence.

Davison took a step toward him, his eyes unflinching, and I swear what I saw in those eyes was the same frozen look of deadly calm that I'd seen when he found Vera and me in the guest room. I'd mistaken it back then for acquiescence, passivity, weakness. I'd failed to sense the fury burning beneath.

Both Monahan and CeeCee reached for their guns at the same time.

Davison never removed his right hand from his pocket. He shot through the fabric of the coat, striking the man in black in his shoulder, his long-barreled gun falling from his hand. Monahan, who was standing no more than a few feet from Davison, took the bullet in the chest, close to his heart. He dropped to his knees in a two-part journey to his demise, then fell face forward on the wooden plank floor.

CeeCee turned to flee, clutching at his shoulder and making his way out the back door onto the deck. Then Davison, hand out of his pocket, pointed the Baretta at me.

He was barely breathing. Face still as stone. A thin band of sweat beading across his forehead.

He held the gun, steady at first then with a slight tremor.

One second. . .

. . .two. . .

. . .three . . .

74

Davison looked from me to the lifeless, sprawled body of Monahan whose flabby cheek was pressed to the floor. A rivulet of blood issued from beneath his shoulder, darkening the wood planks. The man's gum, turned projectile, had landed at the base of the kitchen counter.

Davison lowered the Baretta, said with genuine regret, "I didn't mean for it to turn out this way. I'm not a murderer."

He made his way to the couch and sat with his head bowed, hands between his knees. The gun resting against his leg. "You're the key," he said. "You were then. You are now."

I glanced at the window. No camera. No sign of the clerk. Had the kid at last gone for the police?

"You give me too much credit. Much too much."

"No," the man said gravely. "You stood between us all these years. I tried to pretend that wasn't true. I did everything I could think of to deny it. But I knew. I knew in my heart."

For a time he seemed to drift into reverie. "Every time one of your books came out, Vera would be first in line at the bookstore. She'd go off with the book into some far corner of the house, hole herself up. You couldn't disturb her, you could barely talk to her, for however long it took to read it. Afterwards, when she'd finished, she wouldn't say anything. If I asked her about it, she'd find some way of changing the subject."

I'd always wondered. *If* she'd read them. *If* she'd found herself among the female characters. *If* she'd found echoes of our relationship. I half-expected she'd hated them, though I couldn't have said why. "Maybe she disliked them."

"I don't think so. I don't think that was it at all."

The skin around the man's eyes tightened, his eyes narrowed. "I think they had a profound effect on her. She'd be different for days, sometimes weeks afterward. Not herself, not the Vera I knew." He shook his head in exasperation. "I can't be more precise. I'm not a writer like you."

His eyes had a faraway look as if once again he was forced to watch his shortcomings parade before his eyes, a man humbled by what he perceived were the greater accomplishments of the men around him. "Then *I'd* read the book and make an effort to figure out what had affected her, why she'd become so quiet and moody, what secrets she was hiding from me." He laughed in a belittling way. "Of course I never could figure it out. I don't have an artist's sensibility, or his perceptions."

He looked directly at me then. "I tried to accept, because I had to, that whatever she felt for me was inferior to what she'd felt for you. No matter how much she denied it, no matter how much she tried to reassure me, I knew the most I'd ever be was second best. You have any idea what that feels like?"

I nodded. "I think I do."

His body stiffened, pressed forward. "You *don't*. You *can't*." After a moment, he said in a more tempered voice, "You know where she is, don't you?"

"Yes."

"And you're not going to tell me?"

"No."

"How long have you known?"

"Only since yesterday."

Davison's face seemed about to collapse under the weight of his self-contempt. "You think I'm a fool, don't you? You've been laughing at me all this time, behind my back."

"Believe me, laughter's the farthest thing from my mind."

"Pity then?"

"We're all to be pitied, if it comes to that."

"Is she ever coming back to me?" He said it in such a pathetic, beseeching way that I had trouble reconciling the man's vulnerability with the violent outburst I'd just witnessed.

"I don't know. I haven't spoken to her."

"But you *know*, don't you?" He shook his head in lament. "She's left me for good. Even I know it."

"Anything's possible. You know that as well as I. Maybe she just needs time alone."

Davison spoke slowly, deliberately, as though he'd thought long and hard about what he wanted to say. "A man comes to a point in his life when he sees it clearly for the first time: what it means, what it doesn't mean. How he's been fooled all along, tricked, deceived, how rigged against him it all is: death—the reward for all the time, all the hard work and effort he's put in. Oh, I know we all know we're going to die but it's an abstract thing until the time in our lives when we really *know* it, when we see it straight ahead, no detours, no way out. At that point a man understands the only thing that means anything is having someone to hold onto, to keep him—for whatever brief time is left in his paltry, insignificant life—from dwelling on the oblivion that awaits him."

He sneered at himself, used his free hand to wipe the moisture that was now dripping from his forehead. "Sounds poetic, right? Not the kind of thing you'd expect from a man like me, an associate professor of zoology. I may not be an artist, but what I'm sure of is this: my life was worth nothing before Vera came into it. It's worth nothing if she leaves me."

He sat there rigidly, leaning forward, staring into the room's center, above Monahan's prostrate body.

He stood and leveled the Baretta at me. "Tell me where she is."

"I can't do that."

"Not even if your life depends on it?"

"She wants to be alone now. I have to respect that."

"And what about *me*? What kind of respect do I get?"

Under the circumstances, anything I could say seemed pointless.

"I want you to know one thing," Davison said, lowering the gun. "I didn't go to Monahan; *he* came to me. I didn't want to have anything to do with the man. It was only afterward, when *you* turned against me. When the search became about your finding her for yourself. When you stopped being honest with me. Only then did I accept his offer to help." The agony of that memory seemed to weaken him and his arm trembled, the gun no longer steady in his hand. "I came to you in desperation. I came to you for help and you—" He didn't finish his thought.

"But you were taking a chance, weren't you? You say you knew Vera still had feelings for me. You must have considered things might not go your way."

"Of course, I considered that. But I thought it would be good for her to see you, see you for the self-absorbed artist who wasn't capable of a lasting relationship. *Remind* her of that. I thought that would bring her back to me."

Which reminded me of the words Vera used when she broke it off. Two months after Davison's finding us in the guest room. In that time we'd spoken only on the phone because, as she put it, "she needed time to think, to sort things out." Then one night she showed up in the courtyard outside my apartment. Standing by the fountain. Telling me, over the babble of its rising waters, that it was over.

I can count on him, she said.

And not me?

What we have is wonderful, but—

But—?

How long will it last? What will we have at the end?

We have this moment, now. Isn't that enough?

I don't know—

Of course it is. We have everything. Right now. We're holding it in our hands—

It's what we have in the end that matters, she said. *What endures*. And then, before she turned away, she said: *I just found out today. I'm carrying his child.*

"Besides," Davison was saying, "you were my best hope of finding her and I believed despite your adultery, from everything Vera said, that you were, at least, a man of your word."

"And if I wasn't, you had Monahan in reserve. You had your muscle, if it came to a showdown."

"I told you. That only came later," Davison said.

"The problem, as it turns out, was that Monahan was even more dishonorable than I was. Did you know he tried to get her hooked on heroin? Did you know—?" The horrified look on his face made me stop. He didn't need to hear any more sordid details. I said simply, "You were playing a dangerous game."

Davison's laugh was dismissive. "I knew if push came to shove I could outsmart him. I never doubted that."

We both looked toward the out-of-shape, overweight carcass sprawled across the floor.

"You out-smarted him all right."

Davison looked mortified, his face a combat zone of guilt and revulsion as he tried to process what he'd done, the enormity of it beyond his comprehension. "I lost it. I don't know what came over me."

"It happens."

"I don't understand." The weight of his words fell into the silence of the room. Finally he said, "I expected *him* to betray me. I *planned* for it. But you—"

Once again his eyes had the hard, steely look of the player on the court. Merciless.

The Beretta had found its target once more, staring me in the face. It seemed to have taken on gigantic proportions, looking larger than ever, thrust as it was at the end of his taut, extended arm.

Then Davison withdrew his arm, pointed the gun at his own head, above the ear. "You'll have my life on your conscience. You'll have to live with that."

"For God's sake, Davison—"

He held the gun against his head, both his arm and his hand trembling now. The man gritted his teeth, closed his eyes. "You going to tell me where she is or not? It's up to you whether I live or die."

I considered the options. If the man killed himself, what then? Would I be able to live with myself? I didn't think so.

But I said nothing. I thought he was bluffing.

Davison's finger tightened on the trigger. His arm shook

nearly out of control but the barrel of the gun never strayed from its target.

"*Please*," he said. "Tell me where she is."

The Baretta shivered in his hand.

One second . . . two . . . three.

I swung hard, knocked his arm back and gripped the gun, twisting it so violently it discharged. The bullet striking the window behind us, shattering the glass.

Then his grip loosened and I hurled the weapon across the room.

His body caved in on itself; he sunk down into the couch. In a choked voice he said, "What kind of a man am I?"

He pushed his face into his hands and wept.

Before the police arrived, I wiped clean the .38 I'd brought and flung it into the dense underbrush behind the cabin, thankful I never had to use it.

75

I boarded the small, white ferry from the mainland. After a week of endless interrogations.

After the police had viewed and reviewed the night clerk's video.

After sleepless nights in a one-room Hidden Nook cabin—the Sea Breeze having been cordoned off as a crime scene. The rush of the surf a perpetual whispering presence in the dark.

And after Norm Davison was finally released from custody. After I convinced the night clerk to sign with me a sworn statement saying the shooting had been in self-defense; and after the Chief of Police concluded that, yes, the video showed enough evidence to support that. A search warrant had been issued for CeeCee but thus far at least he seemed to have vanished into that world where hit men like himself dwell while they're waiting for their next assignment. As for the narcotics ring that operated out of the no-name bar in Alphabet City, I decided I'd let that go for the time being, at least until the dust settled. My concern was to get Davison released; I was afraid bringing in Monahan's drug connections would only complicate that.

I didn't want Davison to suffer any more than he had, or *would* in the days to come. I wanted at least to spare him jail time.

The last time I saw him was the day of his release.

On the steps of the courthouse he looked thinner, his cheeks hollowed, his eyes set deeper in their sockets. A man still trying to process the turn of events that had brought him here.

"Does she know?" he asked.

I said I hadn't spoken to her.

"But you will?"

"I hope to."

"Tell her . . . Tell her . . ." His words hung in the air. "Tell her I'll be at home—" His eyes held mine for a long, grave moment before he turned away.

I offered to drive him to his car which had been left at the Hidden Nook but he waved away the offer with a flick of his hand.

Now as the ferry left the slip, I observed the half-dozen fellow passengers. One of them might be on my trail. Or so I imagined, as if Davison or Monahan's crew back at the Madison Houses hadn't yet given up their quest.

I couldn't shake the feeling that an anonymous enemy would always be at my back. Which probably had more to do with those childhood wanderings of mine into crime-ridden neighborhoods than anything realistic. Those ill-advised excursions and the bad dreams that followed—nightmares where I was fleeing down alleys, dark tunnels, bleak empty basements with a dark, menacing male figure following me, a face never revealed. Probably the reason, it had occurred to me more than once, why I became a crime writer. The secret hope I'd eventually find who or what was after me.

But taking the time to study my fellow passengers on the small ferry eased my concern. At least for the moment. They looked innocent enough. Tourists most likely, and a few island residents returning home.

The ferry chugged its way through the inlet, past dockside restaurants, and blocks of identical condominiums, white-shingled units with balconies and black shutters, rising in rows to the top of the ridge.

Gulls trailed the boat like plumes of smoke, but once the ferry cleared the inlet and was riding on open water the birds scattered and flew off, the small craft moving forward alone.

The horizon an immense, unbroken line before me.

76

Holding to the boat's railing, I watched the island take form in the shimmering sunlight. A low green rim rising above blue water. Trees, rocks, thin strips of beach.

At the edge of a marina, a small pier served as the landing dock.

For the moment, as I passed through it, the marina was unattended. Beyond it, a grassy clearing with tables outside a café. A hand-printed sign on the café door read, *Open 5 p.m.*

Farther back amid tall pines: three small cabins, and still farther back an over-sized corrugated tin shed for boat repair and storage. The only worker I found there was a small, dark man, his eyes sunken in a face overwhelmed by wrinkles. He didn't seem to understand, mumbling something incoherent, when I said I was looking for someone.

The island, I would learn later, was inhabited mostly by descendants of the original slaves who tended the indigo plantations that once thrived there. Unsure what to expect, I followed a single narrow dirt road threaded into a forest of dense and dark trees. Every so often a break in the trees, a house sitting in the middle of a clearing. They were small wooden structures, usually white, with eerie blue shutters believed to ward off evil spirits. There was a simple one-story church with a white steeple and a one-room clapboard schoolhouse with a picket fence. No one around, no one to ask.

At the end of the road an abandoned golf course stretched along the sea-edge, a business investment gone bust.

I stared at the empty fairways. The grass already turning brown in the early summer heat. The sea rising beyond.

Beauty and desolation both.

A strange land, to be sure. Thirty minutes from the mainland, but a universe apart.

Where was Vera?

I didn't want to believe I'd been set up again. Fate wouldn't take me this far, and no closer. I felt sure of that.

And then I found her.

At the marina. Past five when I reached it. Music coming from the open door of the café.

She sat at one of the outdoor tables, her back to me.

I stood at the edge of the clearing.

Waiting.

Until the pounding of my heart subsided.

77

Dressed in a pale blue sweater and jeans, her hair pulled back in a pony-tail, she was studying a series of photographs—8x10 color prints, landscapes and seascapes—which were spread across the table.

"No more lovers?"

She looked up then, smiled. "It's simplicity I'm after right now. Trees. Clouds. Surf. Boats nestled in a marina."

"That mean you've given up on love?"

"Taking a break. Re-appraising, you might say. And you?"

"Finding my way. It's taken a while."

"It does. It takes a while." Her gaze was soft, level, some of the light gone from her brown eyes.

"You're not surprised to see me?"

"Sue said you would come. She said you'd been *unyielding* in your pursuit." Then her eyes narrowed in concern. "Your face. What happened?"

Gingerly, I touched my bruises. Still sore, still healing. "Lots of folks looking for you."

"The damsel in distress." She shook her head with regret. "Except my distress wasn't the kind a knight in shining armor could save me from. Only *I* could do that."

I waited a moment taking in the stillness, the grassy lawn, the empty tables around us, the cabins silent among the pines. The ferry horn sounded, an admonition to board. On the pier, several people hurrying toward it.

I told her what had transpired at the Hidden Nook cabins.

When I finished, she was visibly shaken, her face drained of all color. I asked if she knew her husband owned a gun.

"Certainly not. I wouldn't have allowed it, if I knew. Not with Devon in the house."

"We all have our secrets," I said.

"I knew once in a while he went to a practice range. I don't know, I guess I thought he borrowed a weapon, or rented one."

"Of course, it may have come after you'd gone." It seemed inconsequential now, so I said, "I don't know how much Sue told you about what was going on. But I'm still trying to figure out your husband. There were these photographs—violent/erotic ones—mixed in with the others on your desk. Different style really than yours. I wondered if he had taken them, another hint of his dark side. Or maybe you had—"

She seemed disturbed at the suggestion. "All my photos were about small blessings. Specifically, the kindnesses embedded in every touch and kiss and look that lovers exchange. If you want to know the truth, and I'm a little embarrassed to say it, I wanted to show what *our* love—*yours and mine*—was like, what we had and lost."

She shook her head in bewilderment. "So, no, they weren't mine. Norm had a camera, he did take pictures, but like the shooting, it seems so unlike him. Most of the time he was mild-mannered, even-keeled."

"Except on the basketball court."

She looked as if she didn't understand.

"He played hard," I said by way of explanation.

She was thinking deeply about something, her eyes scrunched the way I remembered them when she got serious, head bent forward, small creases on her forehead. "He wasn't into porn, I'm pretty sure of that. And he was a timid lover. More often passive than not."

She blushed saying that, thought a moment before adding, "Except once. That night he caught us. He made me phone you, remember? To assure you I was okay. But then in bed he was brutal and aggressive. It wasn't exactly rape, I didn't try to stop him, but I came close."

I recoiled from the image.

"It's easy," she said, "to miss things in a marriage.

There's so much going on. I spent most of my time and energy caring for Devon. There's a lot Norm didn't know about me. But there was a lot I didn't know about *him*." Her sigh, heavy with regret. "I felt so guilty about leaving him this way—"

"Couldn't you have simply divorced him?"

"He would never agree to a divorce. He made that clear, abundantly so, time and again. The first time—that first time was the day he found us together. To his way of thinking, he told me, marriage was for life, no matter what happened along the way." She looked at me in that old familiar way that said she wanted me to understand, needed me to. "And he was the one who handled our finances. I had almost no money of my own. I'd been through the loss of my son, the only child I'll ever have, and after the struggle of rehab, of getting straight, I didn't have many choices. So when Sue arranged this—this *opportunity*—I took advantage of it. I thought it would be less painful for both of us if I just slipped away. Norm could blame it on Devon's death or my drinking or my erratic behavior. Whatever he wanted to blame."

She lowered her head, considering something. "When I came out of rehab, I was feeling pretty strong. But at times, nights mostly, when the sadness brought me low, I started to doubt myself, this fortress of strength I'd built around myself. And then, that night at the bar when I came so close, I got really scared. I was sure if my life didn't change, I—"

The ferry horn sounded again. The small boat chugging back away from the dock. Her gaze following it as it moved into open water, heading toward the mainland. "Norm will be better off without me."

"He doesn't see it that way."

"We don't always know what's best for us. That was one of your mantras, remember?" Her eyes narrowed as she watched the ferry grow smaller on the horizon. "Besides," she said. "He *knew* I was going to leave him, with or without a divorce. I told him that more than once. He was a master of denial. So none of this should have come as much of a shock."

One more piece of information he'd denied me.

For a while neither of us spoke.

I was deciding in what ways she'd changed. Her hair was longer, bleached from the sun. Her face, when she wasn't smiling, seemed harder and tighter. Age lines that hadn't been visible in the photo had deepened around her eyes and mouth, but she was still unmistakably Vera. More tempered but the enthusiasm in her eyes, if dimmed, had survived. She seemed more centered, less volatile than I remembered.

"One thing I'll always regret," she said, "is sending more of that poison out into the world. I wish there'd been some other way." She drew a long breath and exhaled slowly. "That's something I'll have to live with."

"It didn't sound like you. The woman you've become."

"We don't truly know who we are until we're pushed to the edge, do we?"

I said nothing. At that moment, I wasn't in the mood for passing judgment. I had too many regrets of my own.

She suggested taking a walk. She collected her photos in a neat pile and left them on the table. "Walking helps me process things," she said.

78

Vera guided me toward a path through the pines. She pointed to the first of the cabins with its pitched roof and screened porch. "That's mine."

"Why here?" I asked. "This place. This island."

"Because." She said it as if I should know her reasons. "It's beautiful. It's only twelve miles from the mainland, but it's so much its own unique entity, a different world. And I feel safe here."

"Like at Mercycrest."

She seemed only mildly surprised. "You found my sanctuary?"

"Yes."

"I didn't know if you ever thought of me anymore," she said. "The male characters in your books always seemed so ambivalent about the women they loved. I didn't know if you harbored even a shred of feeling for me."

"I didn't know if you ever thought of *me.*"

"It wasn't until Sue told me about what you were doing to find me that I decided to reach out on the radio. I knew you listened to the program. I'd read that somewhere about you, so I took the chance you'd be listening that night."

"I liked what you said. Love *does* have to be earned. And I didn't earn it. Back then."

"You were too much *in* love. We both were."

We walked for a time in silence. Past the cabins. Past the boat maintenance shed. A gravel parking lot was home to a row of bikes, golf carts, canoes stacked in layers on a metal trailer. "No cars allowed," Vera said. "Which, as you can imagine, slows life down immeasurably."

When we reached the road that curled away through the forest, she told me how much she liked the quiet here, the stillness. "We do get day-trippers," she explained, "hikers and kayakers and the fishing crowd. They're out of here, though, on the last ferry at six and the place returns to its quiet, unpretentious self."

In the late afternoon light, her eyes flared with their familiar youthful fire, the glow of energy and light that had first drawn me to her. "What I'm most excited about, though, is the grammar school. It's really small, only eighteen children. They're going to let me teach them photography three afternoons a week. I've already met them, the children. They're so beautiful. They make me feel so much steadier than I've been."

"You seem pretty steady. You *look* like you have things under control."

"Sometimes," she said. "Sometimes I do."

She looked ahead at the streaks of sunlight through the trees: golden bursts of radiance against the varied greenery of leaves, the stoic brown of the trunks. "There's a spiritual quality here I can't quite put my finger on," she mused. "I'm trying to capture it in my photos."

She thought a while before saying, "There's a day beauty, and a night beauty. By day there's the almost constant brilliance of the sun. At night, though, it's so dark it feels like nothing exists beyond yourself. Yet, for all that darkness, you see yourself in a clearer light."

79

"For a long time I felt like I was living two lives," she said over dinner.

The café windows opened to the wide expanse of sea and sky. The plain wood-paneled room filling with families of locals.

"There were two me's. The one who functioned day to day, being a wife, a mother, trying to move forward with my life; and the one who kept clinging to *us*, what I'd given up."

She had let her hair down and now she fidgeted with it, pulling it back on one side, over her ear. "Until Devon died. And I went to pieces."

She laughed at herself. "*Going to pieces*. Such a curious phrase. Don't you think? What does it mean, really? That you break into fragments of yourself? That the whole *you* dissolves into smaller parts? But what *is* the whole you? What is it exactly that breaks apart?"

"The ultimate mystery," I said. "The self. The one we spend our entire lives trying to solve."

"In my case," Vera said, "I was already split apart, divided, not whole. For me, I guess it meant I couldn't find much of a reason to keep on living."

She settled back in the seat and offered me a thin smile. "But, of course you do. Go on living, that is. You find a reason. Hope returns like a lost friend. I had my art, I had my photos. And the funniest part—funny-weird, that is—the hope I re-discovered came out of that despair."

She barely stopped for breath, talking in that wave-like gush typical of the woman I remembered. "Because bad as that period of my life was, it was the beginning of my acknowledging the other me. The one I'd been running away from all these years. The me I used to be, when I was happy. In college and with you, our brief time together. The artist looking for her truth in a world spilling over with promise. The me I didn't want to let go of. The me I didn't know how to save."

Laughter erupted from a table adjacent to ours, a festive group of islanders joking and laughing among themselves. On the jukebox, a gravelly-voiced man—to the accompaniment of a single guitar—sang of love's age-old miseries: heartbreak and pain, memory and desire. *Before the heartbreak there's love*, was a line he kept repeating. The consistent rasp of his voice comforting despite its sorrow.

I said to Vera, "Is that who I'm talking to now, *that* me?"

"Mostly. As I said before, it's still a struggle. Because to be this me means facing some hard facts. Like how much I've lost. How far I still have to go to get to the happiness I once had. And the hardest thing of all: that I might *never* get to it again, might not even get close. No matter how much I try. Because so much of that fervor, that hope, was a function of youth, denied to me now."

She was silent.

The jukebox silent now, too.

The only sound the wind's murmur beyond the windows and, here inside, the clinking of glasses and silverware. Voices and laughter from the tables around us. The small sounds of night.

"Drinking only made it worse," she said. "Kept me away from what I was trying to get back to. It was my vanishing acts, taking refuge at the campus, that made me sober, made me see there might be a way out, a way ahead. I spent a lot of time in the chapel. *Thinking*, not praying. I took long walks by the river. A lot of meditation. Yoga, too."

She was watching me now, the steady gaze of my eyes on her. "And you?"

And me.

The question I'd spent ten years trying to answer.

I finished off the whiskey in my glass.

Where does one begin?

"So much I didn't know." I let myself appreciate the enormity of that statement. “About love, for example. That it meant so much more than *being* in love, that it was part of a lifetime’s chain of events of which ecstasy was only the smallest part. Your husband understood that, I think. That’s why you went back to him.”

But that was only part of it, I knew. The mystery seen only in fragments. Other parts yet to be discovered.

“You saw something in me I didn’t. Woman’s instinct, whatever. You saw a guy who, over the long haul, is able to communicate deeply on an intimate level only with a sheet of paper, the words I scribble there.”

“Maybe you just needed time to grow.”

“Maybe,” I said.

At least it was a comfort to think so.

She searched a moment for the words. “It’s about working our way back. From the grave we each dig for ourselves.”

80

The marina, at dusk.

The sky a fading lemon color in the west. The metallic clink of the rigging beating against the growing thrust of the wind.

"Along with teaching school, I'll probably volunteer as a tour guide at the Praise House," she told me. When she saw I didn't understand, she added: "It's a one-room stone house. Centuries old. What the slaves used as a place of worship before they had their own church. You can still feel their passion in the walls, locked inside."

"That spiritual vibe you were talking about."

"Yes."

We stood at the edge of the dock, facing the sea. The salt air cooler, damper now. The wind whipping the water beyond the pier to a white-waved frenzy. The rigging clanking hard against metal.

"You worked so hard to find me," she said. "I appreciate that. I do."

"Second chances."

"I don't understand."

"I had to know if they exist."

"They do, *some*times. Though not always in the way we imagine." She waited, before adding: "That's why I put off contacting you. Too afraid, I guess. That you stopped caring for me, that our time had passed. And I wanted to be more settled, *stable*, when I did finally see you."

She was looking toward the barely visible lights of the mainland. "You were right about one thing," she said. "It's what we have in the moment that counts. There's no way to know what we'll have in the end."

We watched night gather over the water.

A restless tide rising and falling against the pylons of the pier.

She leaned against me. Tentatively. “What’s left for us?”

81

In her one-room cabin with its smell of old wood, beneath the over-arching branches of the pines, we made love. A slow intertwining of arms and legs, a determined movement of hands toward what lay beyond our reach. Outside the cabin impenetrable night and the long dark of ocean.

We both knew we were saying goodbye to what we once were.

These are things we understood but didn't say:

We would always love one another for what we were, what we had.

But that love had been borne of a particular time and place and set of circumstances; those two people no longer existed.

And though I had come to understand what I didn't then, that I wasn't that man with so narrow a view of love, she too had moved far beyond the woman she once was.

We would, in so many ways, be starting over.

Not quite strangers, not yet friends.

"Our young, heedless selves," she said, beside me in the dark. "A world that was ours alone. Sometimes I can still feel it. Only a moment, though. Now and then. Here and there. Then it's gone." Her arms, her small delicate wrists, held me tight. "Where does it go?"

"One more mystery we live with."

"Yes."

"I'll come visit," I told her.

"Yes," she said, "I'd like you to."

82

In the morning I stood on the deck as the ferry's engines grew louder, the small boat rumbling as it backed away from the dock. At the edge of the marina, Vera stood alone and gave a simple wave of her hand.

Then she was a receding figure, growing less distinct, the churning water of the ferry's wake carving a long thin line between us.

EPILOGUE

July, 1995

. . . And that, dear listeners, is yet one more of the eight million stories unfolding here in this great city. Until tomorrow, when the dark hours return, this is the Nite Hawk asking you:

What do we do with the night?

Philip Cioffari is the author of the novels THE BRONX KILL; DARK ROAD, DEAD END; CATHOLIC BOYS; JESUS-VILLE; IF ANYONE ASKS, SAY I DIED FROM THE HEART-BREAKING BLUES; and the story collection, A HISTORY OF THINGS LOST OR BROKEN, which won the Tartt First Fiction Prize, and the D. H. Lawrence award for fiction. His stories have been published widely in commercial and literary magazines and anthologies, including *North American Review, Playboy, Michigan Quarterly Review, Northwest Review, Florida Fiction*, and *Southern Humanities Review*. He has written and directed for Off and Off-Off Broadway. His Indie feature film, which he wrote and directed, LOVE IN THE AGE OF DION, has won numerous awards, including Best Feature Film at the Long Island Int'l Film Expo, and Best Director at the NY Independent Film & Video Festival. He was a Professor of English, and Director of the Performing and Literary Arts Honors Program, at William Paterson University. He now teaches for Gotham Writers in New York City. http://www.philipcioffari.com

PGIL2023USA